MW01181684

The Other Place

By
Henry A. Craig

Providing Quality, Professional
Author Services

www.bookmanmarketing.com

ISBN: 1-59453-646-5

DEDICATION

This novel is dedicated to my wife Nancy for her critiques, suggestions, and support. A special thanks to Barb Evenson for her help with the computer and to my brother, Will for editing.

INDEX

CHAPTER ONE

The ten-story Baldwin Building was located in the heart of the downtown business district.   B.G. Baldwin and his two partners, Birdy and Sharpy, had it built with ill-gotten gains from a life of crime.

The three were lifelong friends and had been partners ever since they were young boys growing up together on the streets of the big city.   They had been in and out of trouble of one kind or another most of their lives, and they had been in jail several times.   At one time they had served a prison sentence together for attempted robbery. When they were released from prison the last time, they vowed to play it smart and convert their money from crime into a legitimate business so they could eventually get out of crime altogether.

So far, they had amassed a considerable fortune, but it never seemed to be enough. They always wanted a little more.

Their office was located on the top floor of the Baldwin Building, overlooking the City Park to the north. Their office was the center of operations and it was furnished with the best that money could buy. Next to B.G.'s desk stood a six-foot suit of armor displaying the Baldwin coat of arms. On one wall there was a showcase of exotic butterflies from around the world, with a butterfly net hanging on each side. On the other side of the room they had a wet bar, complete with all the equipment. The bar was stocked with every type of liquor imaginable. A large tournament-sized pool table occupied the middle of the room. Each one of the three men was an excellent pool player. At one time, Sharpy had considered taking up pool professionally but had decided instead to stay with his two friends. A lot of money had changed hands on that table between their pool club members on tournament nights and on several other occasions. Several large photographs and some expensive oil paintings decorated the walls. The two flower stands had fresh flowers placed on them by the florist each morning. Sharpy thought this added an elegant touch to the office.

B.G., as his friends called him, stood looking out the office window at the City Park below. He is in his early fifties, of average height, overweight, and well dressed in an expensive suit. His dark mustache covered a small scar he had received during a knife fight in his younger days. His warm, pleasant smile was deceiving because underneath he was ruthless, vicious, and would stop at nothing—even murder—to get what he wanted. People that knew him viewed him as arrogant, self-centered, stubborn, short-tempered, and greedy. His whole ambition in life was to have it all and to share some of the wealth with his two lifelong partners, Birdy and Sharpy.

Birdy is in his late forties, of average build and height, dull-witted, bungling, and comical. If anything could be screwed up, Birdy would do it. Even if there was no way to screw something up Birdy would somehow manage to screw it up. He would carry out any order B.G. or Sharpy gave him, and never consider the consequences of his actions. Seldom thinking for himself, he accepted everything he was told to do without question. About the only interests he had in life were gambling and his pigeons, which he kept on top of the office building. He got the nickname Birdy because he spent most of his time with the pigeons.

Sharpy is good-looking, in his late forties, and slender. His dark hair and eyes accented a small mustache. A very good dresser, he always wore the best clothes that money could buy. He was smart—far more intelligent than his two partners. The nickname Sharpy came from his being such a sharp dresser and so intelligent. He gambled and bet a lot of money on sports, especially football games. He loved women and was considered quite the ladies man.

Sharpy was seated before B.G.'s desk, totally engrossed in the sport section of the morning newspaper. Birdy was busy building a house out of playing cards on the pool table and listening to rock and roll music on his portable radio.

"Birdy <u>shut that damned thing off</u>!" B.G. roared. "You know how I hate rock and roll music!"

"I think it's sort of nice," replied Birdy.

"I don't care if you do think it's nice. Shut the damned thing off!" B.G. barked

"I'll turn it down. It's nice music," argued Birdy.

"That ain't music! It's a lot of high-pitched screaming and yelling. All those singers sound like they've jerked their shorts up too tight," bellowed B.G.

Birdy shrugged his shoulders and tossed his playing cards down on the pool table. He leaned over to the radio and turned the volume down, but it could still be faintly heard.

"I said turn it off! Completely off!" B.G. shouted. "It's enough having to be the brains around here and do all the thinking for the three of us without having my nerves jangled with that <u>damned screeching</u> and <u>yelling</u>!"

They were interrupted by the voice of their secretary on the intercom. "Mister Marsden is here to see Birdy."

"Tell him I'll see him next week; I'm busy and don't want to be interrupted," Birdy replied.

"Go ahead and send him in," B.G. roared.

Birdy shrugged his shoulders and looked distinctly displeased at having to meet with Marsden.

"Birdy! Quit fooling around with those damned cards and take care of your business," B.G. snapped.

"Well, you don't have to get so grouchy about it," Birdy complained.

Shortly thereafter the door opened and Mister Marsden strode into the room. He wasted no time in going straight to Birdy, who was once again busy with his house of cards.

"Birdy, you owe me thirty-nine hundred dollars and I want my money now!" snapped Marsden. "If you don't want to pay off your football bets, then quit betting on losers and pick a winning team for once."

Birdy looked up in surprise. "I just paid you—I think."

"That was in October," Marsden informed him. "This is January!"

"That was only a month ago," Birdy said, staring into space. "No, two months ago. Now, let's see. Thirty days has September, April, June…"

"Quit your stalling and pay the man, "B.G. demanded.

"I was just trying to figure it out," Birdy mumbled under his breath.

Birdy wrestled a large roll of hundred-dollar bills out of his pocket and started peeling them off one at a time, placing the bills in Marsden's hand.

"There you are," Marsden said, handing the slip of paper to Birdy. "Do you want to place another bet on the Falcons?"

"No! Just mark it paid," Birdy demanded, holding out the slip of paper. "You ain't going to collect twice on me. I may be dumb, but I ain't stupid."

Marsden took out his pen, marked the slip Paid in Full, and handed it back to Birdy.

"Did you make the change in the floorboards of my sports car?" Birdy asked.

"I sure did. Now it's bullet proof too."

"Good! I don't want some lunatic throwing a bomb under my car and filling my butt full of splinters," Birdy chuckled. "With all the lunatics running around nowadays, you never know."

"I don't think lunatics are what you'll have to worry about," Sharpy asserted, peering over his newspaper.

B.G. was still looking out of the window. He leaned over and swung the window open wide. Birdy's card house disintegrated as cards flew in every direction.

"Son of a bitch!" Birdy yelled, grabbing at the cards.

"Whew! It's damned windy out there," B.G. exclaimed as he slammed the window shut.

"No wonder. There's nothing between us and the North Pole but a couple of barbed wire fences," Sharpy joked.

"Yeah, and somebody must have left the gate open," Birdy growled.

"I don't see any of your pigeons flying, Birdy," B.G. said, poking his head out of the window again and scanning the sky.

"I know. It's so windy one of my pigeons laid the same egg three times this morning," Birdy said with a chuckle as he picked up more cards.

"I'll be going now," Marsden announced. "Birdy, you'd better get another bet down. I like that easy money."

"I ain't betting any more. At least not on those damned Falcons," replied Birdy. "I'm going up on the roof to check on my birds."

After Marsden and Birdy left the room, B.G. sauntered over to Sharpy and in a low voice asked, "Did you get the orchestra, dancers, and entertainers lined up for tonight?"

"Sure thing. Everything is set," answered Sharpy. "I explained to the ladies—they are to do a lot of dancing and they're to keep asking the guys to dance too."

"Good!" exclaimed B.G. "Tonight is the big night and I want to make sure everyone has a good time."

Sometime later, Birdy came into the office carrying a white pigeon. He was stroking the bird and talking to it in a low, soothing tone. Going around behind the bar, he slowly slid the cooler door open and took out a six-pack of beer, which he set down on the bar.

"Now, you stay right here and be a good little bird," Birdy said, as he set the pigeon down next to the beer. "I have to get the cans of beer pulled out of the holder."

The pigeon was quiet as Birdy pulled five of the cans from the plastic holder. In his struggle to free the last can, his hand slipped and knocked the other cans of beer off the counter onto the floor. The flying cans and the commotion startled the pigeon, and it took off flying around the room. Birdy dashed over to the wall and grabbed one of the butterfly nets from the showcase.

Birdy yelled to Sharpy, "Grab the other net and help me catch the son of a bitch!"

Sharpy leaped to his feet, grabbed the other net, and the two of them ran around the room, wildly swinging the nets, trying to catch the frantic pigeon. B.G. ducked out of the way every time the two came charging past him swinging the nets.

In their reckless chase they knocked over B.G.'s desk lamp, the flower stands, three chairs, knock seven pictures off the wall, and broke a whole section of stacked glasses behind the bar.

"Where did he *go?*" Birdy asked when he lost sight of the pigeon.

"I don't know," replied Sharpy. "He just disappeared."

The two went creeping around the room with their nets cocked, looking for the bird.

"The last time I saw him, he was over by that big chair," Sharpy said.

The two men crept over to the chair, slowly knelt down, and looked under it. As they did, the frightened bird leaped out from under the chair and took off again, flying around the room, trying to escape.

"There he goes!" Birdy shouted.

Birdy jumped to his feet and landed on a can of beer, causing it to spew all over the expensive carpet. Sharpy was still kneeling and got a blast of beer on the seat of his pants. In anger, he leaped to his feet and started toward Birdy.

"Damn you, Birdy, I don't need a beer enema!" Sharpy snapped, his eyes narrowing and anger showing on his face.

Birdy snatched a cushion from the chair and started backing up, holding the cushion in front of him like a shield.

"You clumsy ox! You just ruined a six-hundred-dollar suit," Sharpy snarled.

Sharpy kept advancing and Birdy continued retreating, holding the cushion in front of him.

"Now, stay back. I don't like that look on your face. Stay away from me," Birdy kept saying.

Sharpy grabbed Birdy by the tie and jerked him up onto his tiptoes, making it hard for him to speak.

"I should punch both of your eyes for this," Sharpy growled.

"No, no. I wouldn't do that," Birdy squeaked. "I don't look so good with black eyes."

"This suit cost me six hundred dollars and I'm taking it out of your hide, bird-brain!"

"Now, let's not be hasty. Here, I'll pay for the suit," Birdy croaked as he fumbled in his pocket for the money.

Sharpy let go of the tie and Birdy settled back down on his feet. While rubbing his neck with one hand, he hastily dug into his pocket with the other and came up with a roll of bills. He peeled off six bills and waved them under Sharpy's nose. Sharpy grabbed the six hundred dollars, then snatched the roll of bills out of Birdy's hand.

"This is for the interest!" Sharpy said, waving the roll of bills under Birdy's nose.

"Sure, anything you say. Anything at all," Birdy said, relieved at not getting hit.

Sharpy started walking toward the door as he counted the roll of bills he had taken from Birdy.

"Hey! Ain't you going to help me catch my pigeon?"

"Hell, no! Catch the damned bird yourself! I'm going to change and get out of these beer-soaked clothes."

Birdy muttered under his breath, "Boy, what an asshole. Takes all my money and won't even help me catch my bird."

"Hey, you guys," B.G. yelled at the two of them. "We've got a big deal going on tonight, so don't screw up and start drinking and walking left-handed on me. Stay sober! We have to make sure we get to keep those big, fat contracts."

"Yeah, yeah, we hear you," the two replied in unison.

Birdy continued searching for the pigeon. Crouching low, he tiptoed around the office looking for his missing bird. Glancing up at the suit of armor, he spotted the pigeon sitting on top of the knight's helmet, watching him creeping around the office. Behaving as if he did not notice the bird, he tiptoed past the statue and swung the net over the pigeon, capturing it.

"Now, now," Birdy said, untangling his pigeon from the net and stroking it. "Did that mean old Sharpy scare you? I'll take you back up to the roof so you can quiet down and be with your friends."

The office was in a shamble—beer all over the floor, chairs overturned, pictures hanging cocked on the wall and on the floor, flowers dumped, and broken bar glasses at the bar. B.G. displays his displeasure with fists perched on his hips, turning around and around as he looked over the office.

"Birdy! You and those damned pigeons are a <u>menace,</u>" he snorted, his face starting to flush.

B.G. leaned over to his desk and pressed the intercom button. "Margaret, get hold of the building super and tell him to get his crew up here to clean up this office. It's a mess."

"Yes, sir, right away," came the reply.

After Birdy left B.G. remained alone, seated at his desk, pondering the events that were to take place that night at the Baldwin Mansion.

CHAPTER TWO

The Baldwin Mansion was situated on a forty-acre estate surrounded by a seemingly impenetrable eight-foot concrete wall. Hidden TV cameras monitored every angle of the yard and mansion. At night the electronic sensors in the yard were activated and the motion sensor lights turned on. With all the modern security surveillance, the three men felt completely safe. The only entrance to the property was by way of a heavy steel gate, controlled from the security room in the house by the security guard. Anyone wanting to get in had to stop at the gate and get clearance first. While the visitor waited for the gates to open, the security guards watching the TV monitors would carefully scrutinize the person, their vehicle, and their license plate number, then this information was entered in the logbook. If the visitor was expected, the gates would open after positive identification was made. If the individual was not known he would have to state his name and business, then wait for the guard to contact B.G. for clearance.

"Shut off the TV cameras and motion sensors for tonight," B.G. said to the security guard.

"Why? You haven't shut the system down since it was installed."

"Tonight is different. I don't want anyone getting scared if an alarm goes off. Some of the guests are very important dignitaries and I don't want them getting spooked," B.G. informed the puzzled guard.

"Are you sure this is wise?" the guard questioned.

"Yes. Some of the guests will be out by the pool and others may be roaming around the grounds. I don't want any alarms going off."

"If that is what you want, I'll start shutting everything down immediately," conceded the guard, shrugging his shoulders.

"All the domestic help will have the night off," B.G. added. "All the food, champagne, hors d'oeuvres and caviar will be catered by the Baylor Catering Service."

"That doesn't sound very good to me bringing in all that strange help," the security guard argued, a frown on his face.

"Don't worry," B.G. assured him. "Baylor is a good friend of mine and he knows his people. There will be a lot of people around here—with an orchestra, sixty guests and their wives, and people strolling about with drinks in their hands. So don't worry. Everything will be just fine."

The guests that evening arrived in limousines and expensive cars. For the most part they were dressed in formal attire, all the ladies were wearing expensive jewelry.

The orchestra provided atmosphere as B.G., Birdy, and Sharpy were standing near the entrance, greeting the guests as they arrived. In between greeting arriving guests, B.G. checked with his partners to make sure they understood everything.

"Now remember, we're throwing this bash to cover up the payoffs to our faithful public servants," reminded B.G. "It also gives you guys an airtight cover story for the little job you have to do."

"Greasing the palms of all those crooked politicians is costing us a bundle and then some," grumbled Birdy.

"Never mind that," snapped B.G. "Circulate and make sure everyone knows you're here. <u>Be</u> conspicuous!"

"What do you mean, be conspicuous?" Birdy asked with a puzzled look on his face.

"Be <u>NOTICED,</u> you idiot."

"OK! OK! I can do that," Birdy assured him.

"What better alibi could we have than being seen in the company of a senator, a governor, a mayor, a twenty-piece orchestra, and a hundred or so guests," Sharpy said, pleased with the prospect.

"We've got some very important people here tonight, so don't screw up, Birdy," warned B.G.

"I won't. You know me," Birdy replied with a smile.

"That's what worries me," B.G. said, pausing to think. "Now remember to mix and be conspicuous."

"We will," Birdy and Sharpy chimed in unison.

Leaning over, B.G. whispered to his partners, "When the party gets into full swing, slip out of here and take care of that business. Then get your asses back here <u>fast</u> before you're missed."

Birdy turned around, knocking the drinks from a tray one of the waiters was carrying. The waiter blinked his eyes, gave Birdy a disgusted look, then looked down at his soaked uniform.

"Excuse me," Birdy apologized.

Birdy started wiping the waiter's uniform with his hands. Then he jerked the handkerchief out of the waiter's vest pocket and continued to wipe. The waiter's face showed his disgust and exasperation. He snatched the handkerchief out of Birdy's hand and threw it down, then tilted his head back and snubbed Birdy. He stormed off with the empty tray, his nose quite out of joint.

"Well, "Birdy stammered in disbelief. "He doesn't have to get so huffy about it. It was an accident."

"Birdy, <u>you</u> are an accident."

"I ain't either. My mother had me on purpose."

"Sharpy, keep him out of trouble," B.G. said firmly. "I have to go because Senator Anderson is looking at the ant farm. He is going to have a lot of questions about our research."

The ant farm was large, with at least one hundred thousand ants in the colony. It was constructed of glass; ten feet long, and rested on a heavy wooden frame.

B.G. threaded his way through the guests and made his way to the Senator. Senator Anderson was bent down, tapping on the glass and watching the ants trying to attack his tapping fingers through the glass.

"Senator Anderson! Glad to see you again," B.G., said, extending his hand.

"I was just studying your ants," Anderson stated, shaking B.G.'s hand. "They're fascinating, aggressive little creatures."

"They're very aggressive when disturbed," B.G. related. "Your tapping on the glass must have angered them and brought them out to attack."

"I heard you had the largest captive collection of ants in the world. Now I believe it," Anderson added.

"I don't know about that, but there are over one hundred thousand ants in this one display. We have two more large colonies in the laboratory," B.G. stated, looking pleased with the interest Senator Anderson was showing.

"So this is the little fire ant your company is working on," Anderson mused, looking intently at the display and tapping on the side of the glass.

The ants immediately swarmed to the glass, trying to get at the tapping fingers.

"No, sir," replied B.G. "The fire ant is the counterpart to the killer bee. It's illegal to transport fire ants out of their territory down south. These ants are a close cousin to the fire ant."

"Do these ants sting like the fire ants?" Anderson asked, studying the little creatures more closely.

"No. Fire ants have a venomous sting. These ants bite, and they're quite vicious when aroused without being fire ants," B.G. replied. "Both ants have the same feeding habits, so if we get the right chemical combination to work on these ants, it should work on the fire ants."

"Good idea!" Senator Anderson commented, tapping the glass again and watching the ants trying to attack. "If these ants should ever get out of here...It's a good thing they're not fire ants."

"That's for sure," B.G. agreed. "That's why we use these ants for experimental purposes. When we come up with the right chemical combination, the lab boys will go down south to the fire ant territory and test it on them."

"Has the lab come up with anything positive yet?"

"I think we're very close," B.G. replied. "The last two experiments were very successful."

"Sounds good to me," Anderson stated.

"If the next test does as well, the team will head down south to attack the fire ant on his own turf," B.G. added.

"Good! I wish you luck."

"Thanks. Now, how about a glass of champagne, Senator!"

"Good idea. I could use one about now."

B.G. extended his hand. "Then right this way, Senator."

The two men walked off toward the bar through the crowd of dancing, milling guests. Birdy and Sharpy were circulating among the guests, talking to as many people as they could, making sure they were as conspicuous as possible. Eventually they wandered out to the swimming pool to chat briefly to everyone out there. Slowly they worked their way around the pool and back to the house.

Several guests were seated close to the an farm. One of the ladies was rather thin, very we dressed, and wore an expensive wig that w done up high on top of her head. Seated next her was a heavy-set lady wearing a dress wit very low-cut neckline, revealing volupti breasts. She was decked out with expe jewelry, a fancy hair-do, and too much ma Seated close to her was Ted Wheeler, a dressed man drinking a highball from a tall glass filled with ice.

Birdy recognized Ted and decided to have a word with him. He threaded his way through the milling guests and dancers, but in his haste to get to Ted, Birdy stepped on the man's toes, causing Ted to jump up and spill his drink down the lady's low-cut dress into her bra. She let out an ear-shattering scream that could be heard over the orchestra. Leaping to her feet, she slapped Ted in the face, then headed for the bathroom. One of the waiters was pushing a cart by the ant farm when she screamed. It startled him so that he rammed the cart into the side of the ant farm, knocking a small hole in the glass. Shocked, he glanced around and, seeing no one watching, quickly hurried off to the kitchen.

The ants immediately exploited the hole in the ass. Silently they poured out onto the floor. m there, they spread out in every direction. people close to the ant farm started saying " and slapping at their ankles, then legs, arms, and necks as the ants worked their er and higher.

ning the orchestra had been playing a usic from the 40's to the 70's. Now ying a slow song for the benefit of les dancing in the center of the gradually found their way out on r and paraded up the dancers' worked their way higher, they

t
ll
ιs
to
ι a
ous
ιsive
ιeup.
well-

20

bit.   The dancers started to flail their arms, stomping, swat themselves, and wiggle all over. It looked like they were doing a new type of dance. The orchestra leader, looking over his shoulder and seeing the dancers in high motion started waving his baton faster, picking up the tempo.

"Look!" Sharpy shouted to Birdy. "The ants are out and they' re wrecking the party! Go get the vacuum cleaner and I'll find out where they're getting out."

Birdy and Sharpy quickly went their separate ways.   The conductor looked over his shoulder again and started waving his baton faster and faster, trying to keep up with the people on the dance floor.

Before long Birdy, returned with the vacuum, jamming the long metal extension tube onto the end of the hose. He plugged the machine in and started vacuuming up the ants. Birdy was down on his hands and knees vacuuming ants when Sharpy came up and tapped him on the shoulder.

"There was a small hole in the glass. I stuck some tape over it. That will hold them for a while," Sharpy said, watching the dancers wiggling and swatting themselves. He began to giggle.

As usual, Birdy was not paying attention to what he was doing.   Before he knew it, he accidentally stuck the end of the vacuum tube up one of the ladies' dresses. She screamed at Birdy, "Watch where you're sticking that thing, BUSTER!"

"Sorry. It was an accident," Birdy apologized, backing away from her angry glare.

Struggling to his feet, Birdy leaned over to Sharpy and whispered, "I'll bet that gave her a thrill."

While speaking to Sharpy, he was of course not paying attention to where he was waving the end of the long vacuum tube. This time it latched onto the lady's wig, jerking it off her head and exposing her short, frazzled hair. She felt the top of her head and saw her wig stuck on the end of the vacuum tube. She screamed, snatched the wig, and stomped off to the bathroom, the wig dangling from her hand.

By now the band members had started to scratch. Before long, they laid down their instruments and started scratching and swatting themselves as fast as the people on the dance floor.

B.G. came hurrying up to Birdy and Sharpy. "What the devil is going on here? I said be conspicuous, not wreck the party!"

"The ants got out through a hole in the glass," Sharpy answered sheepishly.

About this time, B.G. flinched and started to scratch, "Ouch! Son of a bitch! You guys get out of here and take care of that business. Ouch! I'll get this cleaned up."

The evening was illuminated by a bright, full moon, giving everything a warm glow. Two shabbily dressed vagrants were sitting by a bridge next to the abutment. It was peaceful and quiet except for the crickets and frogs singing their evening songs. The vagrants were content to drink from a bottle concealed in a brown paper sack that they passed back and forth as they listened to the crickets and frogs. One of the tramps picked up a large rock and hurled it into the river. The splash made the crickets and frogs stop singing.

"Shhh!" the first vagrant whispered. "I thought I heard a car coming this way."

The sound of the car grew louder and louder until there was no mistaking it.

"It is a car heading our way!" the second vagrant agreed.

The two men quickly scrambled into the shadow of the bridge as the car drove onto the bridge. The car slowed down, then stopped in the center of the bridge. Two men got out and looked cautiously around. Finally satisfied they were alone, the two walked around to the back of the car to the trunk. The first vagrant carefully climbed out from under the bridge, up to where he could find a large rock to stand on. He cautiously peeked through the railing and observed two men standing at the rear of a Mercedes-Benz. He watched as the men opened the trunk, reached inside, and grabbed a large bundle wrapped in a sheet. Then they struggled to get it out of the trunk and over to the side of the bridge. They paused once more to look around and make sure they were alone before lifting the bundle up onto the railing. They shoved it off and watched as the bundle sank into the flowing river below.

The tramp peeking through the lower bridge railing got a good look at the two men and the car before the rock he was standing on came loose. He and the rock went rolling loudly down the bank. The commotion startled the two men on the bridge. They instinctively jerked guns out from concealed shoulder holsters under their coats and leaned over the railing.

"Hey, you! Hold it!" Sharpy shouted.

The second vagrant dashed out from under the bridge and yanked his friend to his feet. Together they dashed down the riverbank, through the thick willows and tall weeds.

"We'd better get them!" Birdy snapped.

The two men leaped off the bridge and started running through the willow thickets in an attempt to catch the vagrants. They soon realized they would never run them down in this thick growth especially at night.

"Hold it!" Sharpy panted, trying to catch his breath. "We'll never find them in this damned stuff."

When Birdy and Sharpy stopped, they were not more than twenty feet from the vagrants concealed in the heavy undergrowth. The tramps could hear them talking over the gurgle of the river and the croaking of the frogs.

"Yeah, we could have passed them and not even known it," Birdy agreed.

"We're supposed to get back to the party before we're missed, so let's get out of here. We'll find those guys later," Sharpy said.

Abandoning the search, the two threaded their way through the heavy growth, back to the bridge. A short time later, two car doors slammed shut and the engine started. The sound of the car gradually faded as it disappeared into the distance.

"That was the same guy we saw shoot a man," the first vagrant whispered to his friend.

"That's exactly what I was thinking," replied the second bum in a hoarse whisper.

"When I recognized him, it scared me so bad I almost pissed my pants; then that damned rock rolled out from under me and I banged my chin and scraped my face," the first bum said, rubbing his chin and raw cheek.

"Are you hurt bad?"

"No, not too bad. Do you think they're actually gone, or is one of them hiding, just waiting for us to come out so they can get us?"

"They must have gone because I heard two car doors slam shut," the second tramp replied.

"That doesn't mean spit! One of them could have shut his door twice while the other one hid out...Why don't you go take a look?"

"No way! I ain't that stupid. If you want to know, you go look. I'm staying right here and protecting my bottle," the second vagrant said, pulling a bottle out of his tattered jacket with shaky hands.

They passed the bottle back and forth, sharing drinks, and settled down for a long, uneasy night.

"I'll bet that was a body they dumped in the river," the first vagrant said.

"Could be," the second tramp replied disinterested now, a little drunk.

"Maybe we should tell the police," he said, rubbing his sore chin.

"Are you crazy?" the second vagrant blurted out. "They'd never believe us and they'd throw us right back in the slammer, thinking we had something to do with it."

"Maybe you're right," the first vagrant conceded.

"As for me, I'm finishing this bottle," the second bum stated, resigning himself to staying put for the night.

He tipped the bottle up and did not stop drinking until it was empty. He wiped his mouth on his jacket sleeve, then threw the empty bottle into the river. It made a big splash then sank.

"That was stupid!" snapped the first vagrant. "If one of those guys is still around, he must have heard the splash and will know where we're hiding."

They cowered in the darkness, hoping they hadn't given themselves away.

CHAPTER THREE

Now the moonlight alternated between bright light and total darkness as clouds drifted in front of the moon. The Mercedes drove up to the garage, and as soon as it was inside the garage door closed, concealing its passengers from the guests. Birdy and Sharpy got out of the car and peered through the garage window at the sky. Sharpy was satisfied it would remain dark for a little while longer. This would give them enough time to get into the house without being discovered.

"We'd better not go in together," Sharpy said. "You go through the gate by the pool and I'll go through the side entrance."

Birdy nodded in agreement and the two went their separate ways to join the party. When they walked in, everything appeared to be back to normal. The orchestra was playing, couples were dancing, and other guests were involved in idle chitchat with each other. Waiters were serving trays of drinks and hors d'oeuvres to thirsty guests. The guests were readily helping themselves, and enjoying the party as if nothing had happened. B.G. stepped up to the bandstand and whispered in the conductor's ear. The conductor waved his baton and the orchestra abruptly stopped playing.

Outside, the clouds had again obscured the moonlight and it was once again dark. A masked man, dressed in black from head to toe, slowly eased himself up onto the concrete wall that surrounded the Baldwin Estate. In his hand was an automatic rifle fitted with a silencer. A large, black pouch hung at his side from a shoulder strap. He cautiously looked around before making a motion with his hand, and then he dropped to the ground. He crouched down and ran to hide in the nearby shrubs as three more black-clad figures appeared on the wall. Each of them carried an automatic rifle with a silencer and a black pouch hanging at their side. They quietly dropped to the ground, one by one, and ran to the shrubs where the first man was hiding. The four concealed men quietly huddled together, cautiously studying the layout of the grounds. They watched for some time, making sure they had not been detected, before they began to move.   The first gunman took another look to make sure the way was clear, then he motioned directions to each man. One by one, they spread out to infiltrate the house and swimming pool area.

A short time later, three gunmen burst in on the party from different directions.

"Don't anybody move!" the first gunman shouted.

To get their attention and make his point clear, he fired his automatic rifle at the long glass mirror behind the bar. It crashed to the floor, sending glass flying in every direction. Several ladies screamed and one fainted.

"We mean business! Let there be no mistake about it!" the first intruder angrily shouted. "Everyone remain quiet and cooperate, and no one will get hurt. We're going to relieve you of your valuables."

The door leading to the swimming pool swung open. All the people that were poolside walked haltingly through the door prodded by one of the black-clad intruders. The first gunman stepped up to the bandstand next to B.G.

"Everybody on that side of the room!" He shouted, waving his gun and motioning to the crowd. "And hurry it up!"

He raised his rifle and fired a short burst into the ceiling. B.G. plugged his ears with his fingers.

Birdy was upstairs in a bedroom with one of the girls when all the commotion started. He was not aware of the holdup-taking place downstairs until bullets came ripping up through the bedroom floor. He ran to the gun cabinet, grabbed an automatic rifle, slipped in a loaded magazine, levered the bolt to put a shell in the chamber, and flipped the safety off.

"What's going on?" the girl asked in a frightened voice.

"Be quiet and stay back," Birdy said, motioning with his hand.

Birdy opened the door of the bedroom and slowly edged his way over to the stairs. Reaching the stairs and leaning over, he took a quick peek and spotted one of the gunmen. He started easing his way down the stairs, looking for a chance to get a clear shot without hitting one of the guests.

The fourth gunman spoke to the first gunman, "We can take over from here."

"You come with me!" the first gunman growled at B.G. "Get going to your study."

With that, the gunman jabbed B.G. hard in the ribs with his rifle barrel, making B.G. groan and wince in pain. As the two walked to B.G.'s study, B.G. was bent over to one side, holding his ribs.

"All right, people, you'd better listen because I'm not telling you twice!" the fourth gunman shouted from the bandstand. "Form two lines and pass by my two friends here. Drop all your valuables into the pouches, then go to the other side of the room. We want your rings, necklaces, earrings, billfolds, and anything else of value.

Don't hold out or try anything cute and you won't get hurt."

The guests started slowly and grudgingly filing past the two gunmen, depositing their valuables in the outstretched pouches.

The fourth gunman was watching everything. He looked up and saw Birdy sneaking down the stairs with a rifle in his hand. A quick burst from the gunman's automatic rifle sent Birdy rolling down the stairs, dead. Some of the ladies screamed and a couple passed out from the shock at seeing someone murdered.

The gunman waved his rifle at the screaming ladies and shouted, "Shut up or you'll be next! Now you know we mean business, so snap to it and get those valuables into the pouches, or you'll get the same."

The two lines started moving more quickly and the guests started depositing their valuables a lot faster than they had before.

The gunman shoved B.G. through the door of his study. After they were inside, the gunman looked around to make sure they were alone.

"Hurry up and open the safe," the gunman growled.

"I don't have a safe. I keep all my money in the bank," B.G. informed him through moans of pain.

This made the gunman angry, and he hit B.G. across the face with the butt of his rifle. The blow knocked B.G. to the floor, and blood started to flow from his cheek.

"You lying son of a bitch!" the gunman growled. "I know you have a safe, and today must be the big payoff. That's the reason for this big party, so you can grease a few palms."

The gunman swung his rifle toward B.G. and fired a semi-circle of lead around his head, into the floor making B.G. flinch.

"Any more stalling and it will be the last thing you do!"

B.G. slowly struggled up from the floor. "I think I recognize that voice."

The gunman slowly pulled the hood off his head, and B.G. just stared. He couldn't believe his eyes.

"Valletta!" He blurted.

"Yes, your old partner you ruined when you stole my half of the company. I said I'd get even with you someday, and that someday is now. I hear you're putting pressure on Walters to make him sell his business to you dirt cheap."

"You're hearing things," B.G. moaned, rubbing his side and feeling his eye starting to swell shut.

"Am I now? Well, Walters hasn't been seen for a week. What did you do, drop him in the river like you threatened to do to me if I didn't sell out to you?"

"No, no," B.G. said, trying to stand.

"Enough talk. Now find that safe!" Valletta barked, jabbing B.G. hard in the side again.

"I think you broke my ribs," B.G. croaked, gasping for breath and holding his side.

"Quit stalling. Find that safe and open it!" Valletta ordered as he raised his weapon to strike B.G. again.

B.G. nodded his head and waved with his hand in an effort to avoid being struck again. He painfully straightened up and staggered over to the bookcase. B.G. pressed a secret locking device, and a section of the bookcase swung wide open, revealing a large safe.

While they were busy at the bookcase, Sharpy slipped through the door carrying an M-16 automatic rifle. He saw the bookcase standing open and could hear B.G. and Vallette. Vallette had his back to the door and was intent on watching B.G. dialing the combination to the safe; he did not think about keeping an eye on the door. Sharpy kept edging along the wall to get into a position for a clean shot at Vallete without hitting B.G.

B.G. looked up at Valletta and saw Sharpy move into partial view. The surprise at seeing Sharpy must have registered on B.G.'s face because Vallette wheeled around and fired a full burst, stopping Sharpy instantly. Sharpy's M-16 chattered aimlessly as he fell to the floor.

Vallette was furious, and angrily turned on B.G., striking him in the face with the gun barrel. The blow knocked B.G. backward to the floor. Fresh blood flowed from the cut on his face. Valletta jabbed him hard with the gun barrel. "Get up and get it open now!"

Slowly, B.G. got to his feet and started spinning the dial on the safe while trying to stop the bleeding with his free hand. He finally finished turning the dial and stepped back. "There. It's open."

"Step back further while I try the handle, and it had better open or you're dead," Vallette warned.

Keeping his gun pointed at B.G., Vallete grabbed the handle of the safe with his free hand and swung the door wide open. "Well, well, well. would you look at that? A bonanza!"

The safe was stacked; bundles of money on one side and a stack of bulging envelopes on the other. Keeping an eye on B.G., he picked up the first heavy envelope and looked at the name on the front, then peeked inside.

"James Anderson. Hmmmmmmmm...Now, why would you be giving a senator all this money?

He leaned over and leafed through the envelopes. Finding a slip of paper, he picked it up and read it out loud: "Stevens, Allard, Wilcox, Miller, Horn. My, my, my, you have some impressive names here. The mayor, chief of police, governor, director of the EPA, a couple of senators, and some others I don't know."

"You'll never get away with this. Too many people know you swore to get me."

"Oh, yes we will," Valletta drawled. "It'll look like a robbery that just got out of hand. Too bad your friends are going home empty-handed. Now get over here and hand me those stacks of bills, and don't try anything funny or it will be the last thing you do."

Vallette motioned with his rifle for B.G. to move back to the safe and hand him the stacks of bills. B.G. knelt down before the safe and started handing over the bundles of money. Valletta was busy stuffing the money in his pouch and did not notice B.G.'s free hand slowly reaching into the back of the safe. Vallette happened to check on B.G. just as his hand came out of the safe clutching a revolver. The thief's automatic rifle fired an instant before B.G. squeezed the trigger, making his shot go wild.

B.G. slumped to the floor. Vallette finished stuffing the money and envelopes into his pouch as if nothing had happened. Before leaving, he kicked B.G. to make sure the man was not alive. He gave B.G. another hard kick and smiled.

CHAPTER FOUR

The white, spotlessly clean room was dimly lit. It was equipped with the most technologically advanced medical equipment known. In the far corner sat a lone figure, observing the three motionless bodies lying stretched out on individual tables.

B.G. was the first of the three to awaken. At first, he moved very slowly; then with a jolt he sat up. He struggled up, looked around, stretched, and rubbed his eyes, trying to focus on his new surroundings. Being half-awake, he was confused and bewildered, not knowing where he was. Squinting in an attempt to see better, he scanned around the room again but did not notice the lone figure sitting in the far corner. He cautiously ran a nervous hand over his face and body, searching for wounds.

The lone figure in the far corner of the room was very old, slim, with gray hair, and very well dressed. He watched B.G. through his glasses.

"I-I thought...I thought I was shot," B.G. murmured to himself as he searched for wounds.

"You were," a voice said from the far side of the room.

Startled, B.G. jerked his head around and squinted at the shadowy figure standing looking at him.

"Who the devil are you?" B.G. snapped, angry at being startled.

"I am Natas," the figure said approaching B.G.

"What do you want?" B.G. growled.

"Nothing," Natas replied. "I'm here to grant your every wish and desire. Also to make sure you abide by the rules."

"I thought I was gunned down." B.G. said, still confused at his surroundings.

"You were," the old man replied.

"Then I'm dead and this is just a dream," B.G. said, thinking he had it all figured out.

"You died all right, but you're not dead here," Natas said with authority.

"How did I get dressed in this fancy suit?" he croaked, checking himself, and his clothes, again.

"I did it," Natas admitted.

B.G. slipped off the table and waddled to a full-length mirror to inspect his clothes and check for wounds.

"You have many more suits if you don't like that one," Natas said, waving his hand toward a long closet.

"I have?" exclaimed B.G. as he turned and saw the closet full of clothes.

"That's not all you have. Look out the window," Natas instructed.

B.G. hurried to the window and looked out. "That's the yacht I've always wanted!"

"Yes, and it's all yours," Natas said.

"Who are all those people walking around on the deck?" B.G. asked.

"That's your crew. They run the boat and take care of it for you."

B.G. was all smiles, as he turned away from the window and looked at Natas as if he was in deep thought.

"This can't be. I must be dreaming," B.G. said, thinking out loud.

"You're not dreaming," Natas reassured him.

"Then exactly what did you mean by granting my every wish and desire?" he asked, a puzzled look on his face.

"Just what I said. Everything you desire I will give you," Natas answered soothingly.

Just who do you think you' re kidding?" B.G. snapped. "I wasn't born yesterday. There's no place like that."

"There is here," Natas said calmly. "Just try me."

"All right. Give me ten million dollars in gold right here on this table," B.G. said, patting the table he had been lying on.

"Would you like it in gold coins or bars?" Natas asked pleasantly.

"You're stalling. Just give it to me in good old USA gold coins."

"Do you want any particular dates?"

"Just as I thought, you're full of BS and just stringing me along," B.G. growled. "Now quit stalling. Give me any dates."

A huge pile of gold coins instantly appeared on the table. B.G. stared in amazement: then he started to walk slowly around the table, staring at the coins.

"You weren't kidding. You really can do it!" B.G. stammered with joy. "Can you double it? No! No! Triple it?"

Instantly the pile tripled in size. Crazy with joy, B.G. started scooping up coins, tossing them in the air, and dancing around the table.

"Wow! This is fantastic!" B.G. gleefully said, running his fingers through the coins.

"Glad to see you like it," Natas said, a small grin starting to creep over his face. "I'm always glad to see people enjoying themselves".

B.G. paused and turned around to face Natas. "What did you say the name of this place was?"

"It doesn't matter what it is called. You can call it anything you like."

"This has to be heaven! Everything is so good and perfect it couldn't be anything <u>but</u> heaven," B.G. said, looking around with a big smile on his face.

"Good, then that's settled."

"Now I have everything I ever wanted. I had no idea I was so good I'd deserve a place like this."

"That's right, you're getting just what you deserve."

B.G. started to slowly rub his chin and circle around the gold on the table, looking at it as if he was in deep thought. After sometime, he stopped and looked at Natas.

"What's this business you mentioned earlier about obeying the rules? What <u>are</u> the rules?" B.G. asked.

"There's only a few rules you must follow," Natas replied.

"Such as what?"

"I must grant your every wish and desire, even those you are only thinking about," Natas nonchalantly answered.

"Now that sounds like a damned good rule to me; just don't forget it," B.G. chuckled, all smiles. "What other good rules are there?"

The next rule is you can never leave here," Natas flatly stated.

"Are you crazy? Who in his right mind would ever want to leave a place where he can have everything he wants?" B.G. said, laughing. "Back on earth, I would have given my soul for a deal like this."

"You always wanted it all; now you have it. You don't have to do anything here but have fun and enjoy yourself all the time, any way you want. If you want something, just ask me and I'll give it to you," Natas promised.

"What a deal! I still can't believe this," B.G. sighed taking another look around. "I should have come here sooner, instead of busting my ass for that nickel-and-dime crap back on earth."

B.G. moved over to the tables where Birdy and Sharpy were lying motionless.

He looked at them for some time and then asked, "What about my two friends? Can they stay here with me?"

"If that's what you want," Natas replied.

"I do! I do!" exclaimed B.G., excited at the prospect of having his friends with him again.

"Then if that's your wish, I'll consult the computer to make sure they can stay with you," Natas replied.

Natas waved his hand and a computer bank with lights, buttons, switches, and big screen appeared out of nowhere. Natas started pressing buttons, flipping switches, and watching the screen. B.G. studied his new friend as Natas worked on the computer.

After reading all the material that scrolled through on the screen, Natas nodded his head.

"Yes, I see they are in the same category as you; they can stay."

The two woke up with a jolt, sat up in bed, rubbed their eyes, and gawked at B.G.

"Boy, am I glad to see you! I thought we were goners for sure," Birdy said, climbing stiffly off the table.

"We're not goners here. This is heaven and we've got it made, guys!" B.G. cried joyfully.

Sharpy hopped off the table and all three hugged each other, laughing and slapping one another on the back.

"Hey, you guys, look at these threads. I thought I had the best before, but they don't compare to these duds!" B.G. said showing off his new clothes.

"Yeah, B.G., you're prettier than a peacock in heat. So stop your strutting," Sharpy said, looking B.G. over.

"Yeah, he does look a little over primed," Birdy agreed with a chuckle.

B.G. went back to the mirror and gave himself a once over, admiring his new clothes.

"I'll have to say I look real good. No doubt about it," B.G. boasted.

"Hey, what's with all these gold coins?" Sharpy asked.

"They're all mine! So keep your hands off," B.G. warned.

"All yours?" Birdy asked, with a puzzled look.

"Yeah, all mine. I finally got it all; and anything else I want, I can have. All I have to do is ask my friend Natas," B.G. boasted.

"That's really something," Sharpy said, continuing to finger the coins.

"You guys want some gold coins?" B.G. asked.

"Sure, we'd like some," Sharpy replied.

"Do your thing," B.G. said, waving his hand at Natas.

Out of thin air a pile of gold coins appeared on each of their tables. The three jumped for joy, laughed, shouted, and showered each other with the coins as they pranced around their beds.

"Now, how about this place? Didn't old B.G. promise to take care of us? Thanks to me, I got us into heaven. Now we have everything we ever wanted," B.G. said, bursting with pride at his accomplishment.

"Thanks a lot, Boss. You're the greatest," Birdy said.

"That goes double for me, Boss," Sharpy added.

"How many times do I have to tell you guys I ain't your boss!" B.G. snapped. "We're partners, friends, buddies—and don't forget it."

"Yes, B.G." Sharpy consented.

"But you're always giving us orders," Birdy protested.

"Well, someone has to take charge and make all the decisions, and I haven't done so bad so far. Look where it got us. So be thankful," B.G. said.

"Okay," Birdy conceded.

"Do you guys want to have some fun? Maybe some gals, booze, cards, or a party? What do you say? My pal Natas can fix us up with anything we want," B.G. said, excited at the prospect of having a good time.

"Yeah! I feel like a party with lots of booze and some real gorgeous gals," Sharpy said with a smile. "And while you're at it, make the gals like a coke—nice and shapely."

"You want our gals shaped like a can of Coke?" Birdy asked, puzzled.

"No! The bottled kind, you ignoramus!" growled Sharpy.

"I know exactly what you mean," Natas said. "Just how many ladies do you want?"

"A couple apiece should about do it," B.G. said, gleefully rubbing his hands together.

"Make mine raring to go because I need a lot of red-hot loving," Birdy said with a silly grin.

"I thought you swore off women and only liked your pigeons," Sharpy stated.

"Me and women never did get along back on earth, but here in heaven they have to love me," Birdy replied with a smug look on his face. "So bring on the gals; I've got a lot of loving to catch up on."

Six beautiful women strolled into the room, dressed for an evening on the town. Two of the ladies sensuously walked to Birdy and started hugging him and showering him with kisses.

"Now…(kiss)…this is…(kiss)…real living! Hold it, girls, you're getting my damper turned up," Birdy gasped, trying to break away from yet another affectionate kiss.

"Birdy, you can stay here if you want, but as for Sharpy and me, we're going dancing, boozing, and gambling," B.G. said, clapping his hands and doing a little dance.

"Yeah, you guys get lost. I've got an itch that won't stop and lot of catching up to do. I'll see you guys later," Birdy giggled as he put his arms around the girls.

A dance band was blaring away in the distance. The music was coming from the nightclub where B.G. and Sharpy were headed with their ladies. They strode into the nightclub with a lady on each arm.

The club was crowded, and a rip-roaring party was in full swing. The dance floor was filled with couples dancing, and the bar was lined with drinkers. Most of the tables were filled with people drinking, telling jokes, and laughing.

"Yahoo!" B.G. shouted. "This is my kind of party. I'm feeling frisky and ready to celebrate. Just throw me into the middle of that glorious party!"

"Yeah, this is some rip-snorting party!" Sharpy agreed. "Just let us have at it."

"Let's have a couple drinks first," B.G. suggested.

"Sounds good to me, "Sharpy admitted, smacking his lips.

The six threaded their way through the crowd and found an empty table. They ordered a few rounds of drinks and then started dancing. B.G. danced several times with his ladies while Sharpy danced with his. Then they went back to their table and had another drink. B.G. and Sharpy switched ladies and danced some more. They continued to drink and dance until both were staggering and bleary-eyed. All the drinking and dancing did not appear to have any affect on the ladies, who were still as fresh as a daisy and full of life. Another dance and the guys were all done in; they were beat. They staggered back to the table and plopped down, completely exhausted.

"Where the devil is Natas?" B.G. said with slurred speech, looking all around for his new friend.

"Right here!" Natas said in a loud voice from behind B.G.

"Damn it," B.G. snapped. "Don't sneak up and scare me like that again! You nearly gave me fart failure."

"You mean heart failure, don't you?" Natas corrected.

"I mean fart failure! You nearly scared the crap out of me," B.G. guffawed.

"What did you want?" Natas asked politely.

"My feet. They're so sore, I can hardly touch them on the floor," B.G. moaned.

"My feet are killing me too. I never knew feet could hurt so much."

"What is it you want me to do?"

"Fix our feet," B.G. said with an agonizing groan.

Natas waved his hand and the pain left. The two wiggled their toes and stood up, trying out their rejuvenated feet.

"This is great!" B.G. said, happy that his feet were back to normal and the pain was gone.

"My feet are fine. The pain is gone," Sharpy said, trying out his feet.

"How about sobering us up? I'm so drunk, I take two steps forward and stagger back one. I know I must be drunk when my ugly friend here starts looking handsome. He is so ugly, he has to sneak up on the water glass to get a drink," B.G. said jokingly as he slapped Sharpy on the shoulder.

Natas waved his hand and the effects of the alcohol vanished.

"This is great! I feel like a new man. Now I'm not walking left-handed," B.G. exclaimed, walking back and forth, testing his feet and legs.

"Yeah, I feel good too, but it sure is a waste of a damned good drunk, "Sharpy commented.

"I'm tired of dancing," B.G. acknowledged.

"Me too," Sharpy agreed. "Let's do something different."

"How about some gambling?"

"Sounds real good to me," replied Sharpy.

With a lot of laughter and boisterous talking, they left their table and moved to the adjoining room. Sharpy and his two ladies headed for the roulette table. B.G. sat down at a poker table with his ladies standing behind him.

"Give me a hundred thousand dollars in chips," B.G. said with a big smile, rubbing his hands together. "I'm going to break the bank because I'm here to kick up my heels and howl!"

B.G. turned to his fellow card players and said, "You guys might as well give up now and push all those chips over here. That will save you the agony of watching me take them from you one at a time."

All the players chuckled as they eyed this brash, new player.

"He's a brazen son of a bitch, ain't he?" one of the players stated.

"An arrogant bastard if you ask me," another player said, eyeing B. G with contempt.

"Name-calling won't help you, because I'm going to win every hand," B.G. stated flatly.

All the players chuckled again.

Sharpy watched the roulette wheel stop on his number and the croupier push a large stack of chips to him. He raked the pile in and added it to the stacks he had already amassed. Every time the roulette wheel spun, it stopped on Sharpy's number. His pile of chips just kept growing with each spin.

B.G. was still playing poker and having a good time.

"Feast your eyes on that—another royal flush! Sorry, boys, it looks like I win again," B.G. said with a smug look on his face.

"You're the luckiest bastard I've ever seen," one of the players complained.

"It doesn't make any difference what we have; your hand is always just a little better," griped another player.

"Yeah! When you're hot, you're hot," B.G. taunted. "Just keep those darling pasteboards coming."

B.G. was elated beyond belief. He turned to his ladies, who were still standing attentively behind him.

"You gals are bringing me good luck, "B.G. said, smiling.

He took a double handful of thousand-dollar chips and shoved them down each of their bras.

"If I keep on winning, I'll fill up the other side," he said, laughing.

The ladies were very appreciative and gave him a big hug and kiss.

"Cut out playing with the women and let's play cards. We want a chance to get our money back," growled one of the players.

"Just keep your shirt on," B.G. growled. "I'll play some more; I don't have all your money yet."

Sharpy won each time the roulette wheel stopped spinning. He placed his chips on the corners, on odd, even, red, and black. It didn't make any difference where he placed his chips, he won. He won so much, a cart had to be brought in to clear off his winnings so he could continue to play.

B.G. also kept winning, hand after hand. By now he was so cocky he left his cards face down and didn't look at them before calling the bet and raising the stakes. None of the players dropped out. They called his raise and anxiously waited to see what he turned up. B.G. slowly turned his cards over one at a time.

"Well would you look at that—a royal flush. I win again," B.G. crowed. "Sorry, boys."

"Sorry, my ass," quipped an angry player.

B.G. had won so much money a cart had to be brought in to clear his winnings off the table. He looked around, spotted Natas, and waved him over to his table.

"Natas, this is not fun any more. In fact, it sucks!" B.G. complained "Winning every hand isn't the fun I thought it would be."

"You said you wanted to win every hand, and you did," Natas reminded.

"I know what I said, but winning all the time stinks!"

"So, what's the problem?"

"It was fun and exciting at first, but it got old. That was when I started betting without even looking at my cards to make it more interesting," B.G. stated.

"I can fix that easy enough. Just what per cent would you like to lose—ten per cent, twenty per cent?" Natas offered.

"No!" B.G. emphatically said. "That would still be the same, knowing how many hands I would win. If I said ten per cent, I'd know I would lose only ten hands and I'd still win. I'm bored with this."

Sharpy and his ladies strode over to B.G.'s table and sat down.

I don't know about you, but I'm tired of this win, win, win all the time," Sharpy complained.

"Well so am I," grumbled B.G.

"Let's get out of here and do something different," Sharpy suggested.

"Where is Birdy?" B.G. asked, looking around for him. "Has he showed up yet?"

"No, he is still with his ladies," Natas replied.

"Damn! You'd think he would have had enough by now," B.G. said in disgust. "How long have we been here, Natas?"

"There is no such thing as time here, but in earth time I would say a little over ten months."

"Ten months!" blurted B.G. in disbelief. "No wonder this place is getting to be a pain in the ass. Let's get Birdy and go fishing or do something else."

"Anything but this place. I don't want to see a deck of cards ever again. You gals get lost," B.G. said with a wave of his hand. "We're going fishing on my yacht."

Natas followed close behind the two as they strode across the floor and out the door. The three strolled on until they came to the building where Birdy had said he would be waiting. They stopped and waited for some time before Birdy finally came limping through the door. He was bent over, and taking very small steps.

"What's the matter with you?" B.G. asked.

"Ooooh, I hurt all over like a tooth ache," Birdy said. "Those damned women wouldn't leave me alone. No more women for me—ever!"

"Natas, fix him up like you did us so he can move," B.G. said.

Immediately, Birdy straightened up, stretched, flexed his body, and could move normally. Natas waved his hand again and a limousine appeared. The driver got out, opened the door, bowed, and motioned for them to get in.

"This isn't necessary; we can walk. My yacht is right there," B.G. said, pointing. "We can see it from here."

"I know," Natas replied. "It's Birdy's desire to have a limousine ride, so ride."

All four of them piled in and rode the five blocks down to the dock. There, they hopped out and walked down the pier to B. G's yacht. The crew was lined up along the railing to welcome the party as they went aboard. The three men thought it was nice to stand on the deck and look around at the scenery. They just stood there looking for quite some time, waiting, for the yacht to cast off.

"It's your yacht, B.G., so you'd better tell the captain to shove off, or you'll be standing here all day," Natas said.

"Captain!" B.G. shouted up to the wheelhouse, feeling very important. "Let's shove off."

"Aye-aye, sir," replied the captain. "Cast off forward and aft lines. All ahead one quarter standard."

As the yacht slowly started to move, they found deck chairs and made themselves comfortable. They were intrigued by the sea gulls—how little effort they took to stay airborne. Occasionally, a bird would swoop down to catch a small fish, then fly back up into the air again. The steward brought out drinks, and the group relaxed and enjoyed watching the land fade into the distance as they cleared the harbor. As soon as they were out of the harbor, the engines came to life and the bow went slicing through the water, throwing a large spray.

"B.G., what do you want to catch?" asked Sharpy.

"I want to catch a king-size tuna that will break all records."

"Me, too," Sharpy announced loudly.

"No, you don't! I'm catching the biggest fish. You guys will have to catch a different fish," B.G. growled. "I'm going for breaking the record. You guys know how I hate to lose at anything."

"Yeah we know. You always have to win," grumbled Birdy.

Natas was standing in the background, listening to everything they had to say and making notes in a small notebook. Natas had a big smile and appeared to enjoy taking notes.

CHAPTER FIVE

Before long, the noise of the ship's engine slowed as the boat came to idling speed for trolling. The three took off their suit coats, ties, and shirts. They were stripped to their T-shirts and ready to fish. The deck hands brought out fishing rods. The three watched as the deck hands baited the hooks, played out the line, and placed the poles in the rod holders.

"Do you guys see this lever?" the deck hand asked, pointing to the side of the reel.

"Yes," they replied in unison.

"Whatever you do, don't flip it forward. Keep your fingers away from it, so you don't accidentally flip it," the deck hand warned. "If it's flipped forward, that will throw the reel into free spooling, which is used to let the line out. You won't be able to set the hook. The lever must be back to set the hook."

The three nodded that they understood. The deck hand motioned for them to get in the fighting chairs. As soon as they were seated, they started catching fish. They caught and released all the fish they could ever hope for or even imagine.

"Hey, Natas, I'm tired of catching these little thirty-to-forty-pound fish," B.G. yelled over his shoulder. "When am I going to catch my record-breaking tuna?"

"Anytime you want."

"Well, how about now?" B.G. snapped.

He had no more than gotten the words out of his mouth when the big deep-sea reel on the heavy rod, started to spin and sing—the line peeled off at a dizzying pace. Two deck hands ran to the deep-sea rod and jerked it out of the rod holder.

"Get into the heavy fighting chair!" one of the deck hands yelled to B.G. as they ran the fishing rod over to him. "Strap yourself in and put your feet in the stirrups. A fish this size can jerk you overboard."

B.G. scrambled into the chair and Sharpy carefully strapped him in. When he was ready, the deck hands placed the butt of the rod in the swivel socket, handed him the rod, and snapped on the safety line. With a jerk he set the hook hard. The battle was on.

"Wow! Would you look at that line peeling off the reel! It feels like I've tied into a bull elephant!" B.G. yelled, excited. "I can feel the throbbing in the pole every time that monster shakes his head."

He had his feet firmly planted in the fighting stirrups; his body leaned back and his arms were stretched out straight forward, gripping the straining, arched rod.

The battle had been going on for some time when Sharpy spoke up. "You're perspiring a lot."

"And you're sweating, too," Birdy added.

Large beads of perspiration were trickling down B.G.'s face, and his T-shirt was soaked. He was straining every muscle in his body as the rod bent and throbbed under the heavy pressure. Through grunts, groans, and gasps for air, the battle went on as B.G. tried to gain line and reel in the fish.

"Sharpy," B.G. gasped. "Pour some water on me. Birdy get me an ice-cold beer!"

Birdy and Sharpy dashed off and soon reappeared with a pitcher of water and a cold beer. Birdy gave him gulps of beer; in between gulps, Sharpy poured water on his head. The fish leaped out of the water many times, shaking its head, trying to throw the hook. Every time the fish came catapulting out of the water the deck hands applauded and whistled. The fight between man and fish went on and on.

"Natas," B.G. gasped sometime later. "When am I going to land this fish?"

"Anytime you want."

"How about now, before I die from exhaustion?"

The line went slack and the pole straightened. B.G. slumped back in his chair, weak from exhaustion.

"Damn it! He got off," B.G. weakly groaned. "All that work for nothing."

"Don't worry, he's still on," Natas calmly said.

"Bull crap! I know when a fish is off," B.G. said, giving Natas a disgusted look. "You're playing games with me."

"Reel <u>in your</u> line!" Natas ordered in a loud, stern voice.

"Okay, okay. Don't get your coconuts in an uproar," B.G. replied as he tentatively started to reel in the line.

The fish had been a long way back from the boat, and it was going to take some time before he got it reeled in. B.G. slowly cranking the handle until he caught sight of the giant fish swimming on top of the water, headed for the boat. The closer the fish got to the boat, the faster B.G. reeled. Finally, he got the fish alongside the boat, and everyone crowded to the railing to look at his giant tuna. The deck hands lifted the fish out of the water with a power hoist and swung it on board.

"Want your picture taken with your tuna?" a deck hand asked.

"Why not?" B.G. gasped, tottering over to the fish on weak legs.

After his picture was taken, he wanted more pictures, including the three of them and his fish. When the picture session was over, B. G staggered back to his chair and plopped down with a sigh of relief.

"I'm so hot I feel like I'm burning up," B.G. groaned.

"I can take care of that," a deck hand said, disappearing into the cabin.

"You guys go ahead and catch all the fish you want. I'm not getting out of this chair, ever!"

The deck hand reappeared with a large bucket of ice water and dumped it on B.G.'s head. His temper flaring, B.G. jumped to his feet, knocking over the deck chair. "What in blue blazes are you trying to do—drown me?"

"Just cooling you off," replied the deck hand.

"The next time, warn a person before you try drowning him," B.G. angrily snapped.

"Yes sir, I will," said the deck hand before scurrying back to the cabin.

B.G. sprawled out in his deck chair. Birdy and Sharpy were having a good time catching fish. They caught fish of every size, shape, and species. They even caught some prehistoric fish.

B.G. feebly motioned Natas over to him. "Fix me up before I die of exhaustion, B.G. panted. "I guess I can't do that, for I'm already dead...or whatever I am."

You're not dead, just in another dimension," Natas reassured, waving his hand.

"Yahoo!" shouted B.G., stretching and flexing his muscles. "I feel like a new man again!"

"Want to catch another fish?" Natas asked.

"Don't even think it!" B.G. grunted.

Eventually, Birdy and Sharpy got tired of catching fish too. They stumbled over to B.G. and sat down next to him in deck chairs.

"I don't know if you two have had your fill of fishing yet, but as for me, I'm tired of fishing and I don't care if I ever go fishing again," B.G. stated flatly.

"Me too," Sharpy agreed.

"Yeah, let's quit this crap and go do something fun, something different," Birdy said, his boredom reflecting in his voice.

Leaning over and whispering to his friends, Sharpy asked, "Have you guys noticed anything strange about Natas?"

"This whole damned place is strange. Whoever heard of a place where you could have everything you wanted?" Birdy stated. "I think we're having some kind of weird nightmare."

"No! I mean there's something strange about Natas."

"Just what do you mean by strange?" B.G. asked.

"I've been watching him, and every time we get fed up and bored with something, he gets this strange sparkle in his eyes," stated Sharpy.

"You're nuts! This is heaven and angels are <u>supposed</u> to have sparkles in their eyes," B.G.

snapped. "I got us into heaven, didn't I? So enjoy it. We've got it made!"

"Forget about Natas and fishing. Let's get back to shore where there is some real live action," Birdy pleaded.

B.G. cupped his hands around his mouth and shouted up to the wheelhouse. "Hey, you up there in the wheelhouse! Turn this floating hotel around and let's head back to shore."

The captain turned the wheel and the engines came to life. Soon the yacht was under full power, heading for shore. The three fishermen sat quietly on deck, watching the wake as the boat sliced through the water.

A deck hand came out of the wheelhouse with B.G.'s pictures. "Do you want your pictures?"

"Let me see them," B.G. replied, taking the pictures.

He looked through the snapshots and then offered them to Birdy and Sharpy. "Do you guys want to look at them?"

"No, we've seen more than enough fish without looking at pictures of them," Sharpy said, looking the other way.

"I don't want to see them either," Birdy confessed, a frown creasing his brow.

"In that case, I guess nobody wants them." B.G. tossed the pictures up into the wind.

It was not long before the engines slowed and they entered the harbor. The boat docked and the three went ashore. They had trouble making their legs behave the way they wanted, so they tried stretching and some knee bends to get rid of their sea legs.

"Damn! It's hard to walk on solid ground again. The ground doesn't go where my legs want to go," complained Sharpy.

"Natas, just how long did we fish?" Birdy asked.

"Oh, in earth time about three years," Natas replied with a smile.

"No wonder we're having so much trouble walking," B.G. said, grabbing his legs and trying to force them in the right direction.

"You could have fished throughout eternity if you'd wanted," Natas stated calmly.

"No thanks! B.G. said emphatically. "We don't want to look at another fish, or boat for that matter."

"What did he mean by eternity?" Birdy asked.

"What he means is, we could have fished forever and never stopped, you moron," Sharpy said gruffly.

"Well, you don't have to get so huffy about it. I only asked," Birdy replied.

Natas walked some distance from them and sat down on a bench in the shade. He was waiting for them to decide what they wanted to do next.

"Did you see that?" Sharpy said, all excited.

"See what?" demanded B.G.

"I was right about that sparkle in Natas' eyes," Sharpy blurted.

"I didn't see it, and you didn't see it either. It's just your imagination, so forget it!" B.G. ordered.

"I think Sharpy is right. His eyes did have sort of a glowing sparkle," Birdy agreed.

"You guys are nuts! You're starting to give me the willies, so stop it!" B.G. ordered. "What would you guys like to do now that we are on shore?"

"I don't know, "Sharpy half-heartedly replied, still thinking about Natas' eyes.

"I don't care...whatever," Birdy said, shrugging his shoulders.

"How about some archery? I always wanted to try that," B.G. suggested, trying to instill some excitement in his two friends.

"You've never said anything about archery before. Why now?" Sharpy asked, giving him a puzzled look.

"It sounds like it would be fun," B.G. said enthusiastically.

"He wants to be Robin Hood," Birdy joked.

"Yeah, I can just see you now, playing like Robin Hood and trying to shoot an apple off Birdy's head," Sharpy quipped.

"That was William Tell that shot the apple off his son's head, you ignoramus," B.G. corrected.

"You ain't shootin' no apple off my head," Birdy said, clasping his hands over his head. "I ain't that stupid. I didn't fall out of a tree, you know."

"Forget the archery.   Let's play golf," B.G. suggested.

"Sounds real good to me," Sharpy agreed.

"Yeah, let's play a little of that pasture pool," Birdy said eagerly, taking a practice swing like he had a golf club in his hands.

"When we get tired of that, we can play basketball, horseshoes, swim, drink more suds, dance, sky-dive, ride horses and do all sorts of fun things," B.G. cheerfully informed the other two.

The three waddled over to Natas and asked him to fix them so they could walk normal. With a wave of his hand their sea legs disappeared and they were back to normal. The three sauntered off to the golf course—followed by Natas.

Later, they walked out of the clubhouse, carrying their golf bags, and strolled up to the first tee. B.G. pulled a driver out of his bag and took a few practice swings.

"Natas, what is par for this course?" B.G. asked.

"Thirty-six for the course and three for the first hole."

"You guys go first so I can see what I have to beat," B.G. stated.

"You always want to win. Well, not this time because I'm going to par this hole," Sharpy said with a flair.

He teed up the ball, made a practice swing, stepped up, addressed the ball, and took a hard swing. The shot was a long, straight drive down the fairway, and the ball landed squarely on the green. It was a drive that would have made a pro happy.

"How about that for a line drive?" Sharpy said, obviously very pleased with his effort.

"Pretty good for an amateur, but not good enough. Just lay an eyeball on this shot," Birdy boasted.

While he teed up the ball and took a practice swing, B.G. leaned over and whispered something to Natas. Birdy firmly planted his feet, drew back and took a hard, vicious swing. The ball rose about ten feet in the air and exploded with a terrific bang.

"Did you see that? Did you see that?" Birdy shouted. "I hit the ball so hard it exploded!"

B.G. and Sharpy were laughing so much they could hardly catch their breath.

"Ha, ha, ha! You should have seen the look on your face when that ball exploded," B.G. said, laughing so hard he could hardly talk.

"Okay, wise guys. I'll show you clowns this time!" Birdy fumed.

Birdy went to his golf bag for another ball, which he teed up and took a swing with vengeance. The ball took off like a rifle shot for a long drive and then started to curve in a big slice. They watched as it made a complete circle and landed at Birdy's feet. Sharpy and B.G. could not contain themselves. Tears flowed down their faces as they clasped their sides in fits of laughter.

After B.G. regained some of his composure, he could finally speak. "Birdy, if you don't stop hitting those boomerangs, we'll never get off the first tee."

That was enough to send B.G. and Sharpy into another outburst of laughter.

"I haven't had this much fun in years," Sharpy managed to say through fits of laughter.

"You guys wouldn't think it was so funny if someone was screwing around with your balls!" Birdy said in disgust.

That sent the two of them into hysterics, again tears trickling down their cheeks. Sometime later, after the laughter and joking subsided, they got down to the business of golf.

"I guess I'll have to show you guys how it's done," B.G. stated arrogantly as he strutted up to the tee box.

He teed up the ball and yelled back to Natas, "I want to make a hole in one."

He swung hard and the ball made a high arch, landed on the green, and rolled into the hole.

"See! Nothing to it," B.G. said, strutting and bowing as he left the tee box.

"We can do that, too!" Sharpy sneered. "Natas, the same!"

Sharpy made a perfect hole in one. He was followed by Birdy doing the same.

"You guys think you've caught up with old B.G., do you? You're not so smart. Just watch this."

After teeing up his ball, B.G. shouted to Natas, "I want to make nine holes in one."

Birdy and Sharpy looked at each other.

"What's he trying to do now?" Sharpy asked.

"I haven't got the foggiest notion."

B.G. smacked the ball and it took off on a high rise, then dropped in the first hole. It flew out of the cup on its way to the second hole and dropped in. The ball continued around the course, hopping in and out of each hole, until it had completed all nine holes. Finally it rolled to a stop at B.G.'s feet.

"How do you like that?" he said with a conceited laugh. "Let's see you guys beat that if you can!"

"All right, just watch this!" Sharpy said, stepping to the tee box. "Natas, around the course twice, my good man."

He teed up, took a hard swing, and the ball flew around the course twice, leaping in and out of each hole.

"How about that! Eighteen holes in one," Sharpy boasted. "Thought you could put one over on me, did you?"

"If you two think you're so damned smart, just watch this!" Birdy stated.

Birdy nonchalantly walked up to the tee box, teed up two balls side by side, and then nodded to Natas.

"Natas, both balls in each cup and around this turkey farm twice," Birdy said jokingly, waving his driver dramatically.

He took a careful stance, planted his feet firmly, and swung, hitting both balls at the same time. The balls popped in and out of each hole as they flew around the course twice. Finally they rolled to a stop at Birdy's, feet.

"How do you smart alecks like that? Thirty-six holes in one," Birdy said with a big guffaw.

"This is no fun either!" B.G. lamented, a frown on his face. "We can make any score we want without leaving the first tee. Let's quit and play basketball."

"Yeah, I agree. This sucks!" Sharpy admitted. "Let's play basketball."

"You guys want to quit because I beat you," Birdy said, poking a little fun at them. "All right, if basketball is what you want to play, I'm game. I'll beat you at that, too, because I used to be really good at basketball."

"Sure you were," B.G. said, not believing a word of what he said. "You're such a klutz, you can't scratch your ass and walk at the same time."

The three walked off the golf course, Natas following close behind as they headed for the basketball court. When they got to the court, each of them took a ball to practice shooting before playing one on one. To their amazement, they could shoot from anywhere on the court and make a basket. They soon discovered they could not miss. They tried closing their eyes and shooting, but the ball still went sailing through the net. They tried throwing the ball in the wrong direction, but it would come back to the basket and drop through. After they got tired of never missing a shot, they thought it would be fun to try to miss. They bounced the ball off the walls and it went in. They threw the ball up to the ceiling and it went through. When the ball was dropkicked they made every basket, no matter what direction they had kicked it. No matter what they did, they never missed a basket.

"I've had it with basketball!" Sharpy announced.

"I've had my fill, too!" B.G. agreed.

"Let' s go swimming, "Birdy suggested. "I love to swim, because I can swim like a fish."

"Sure you can," B.G. said, doubting him. "You probably swim like a rock, and we'll have to scrape your fat carcass off the bottom of the pool."

For a while they enjoyed swimming. They made any dive they could think up and every one was flawless. Before long, they discovered they could swim at any speed they wanted. Birdy tried to see how fast he could swim under water, and he looked like a high-speed torpedo streaking around the pool.

Tired of swimming they decided to try hockey. The goalie didn't have a chance as the puck repeatedly shot past him like a bullet. They scored from any direction on the ice. Tiring of hockey, they tried playing horseshoes, but made nothing but ringers. They tried to amuse themselves by going horseback riding and sky diving. They even tried archery. They made such perfect shots, they could split an arrow that was already stuck in the bull's-eye. They tried everything again and again, but did not enjoy it in the least.

"We've done everything possible a hundred times and more. Nothing is fun anymore! We're all bored stiff with everything," Sharpy complained bitterly.

"Natas, check your computer again and see if there wasn't a mistake in our being sent here."

The computer materialized again, and Natas started pressing buttons and throwing switches. After a while, the computer printed out a sheet of paper, which Natas tore off and handed to B.G. The three stared at the sheet.

"There is no mistake about it; you boys belong here," Natas replied.

"We don't care what your damned old computer says," B.G. said angrily, as he tore up the sheet, threw it to the ground and stomped on it. "We've had it with heaven; it's too perfect. We don't fit here. We want to go to the other place!"

"THIS IS THE OTHER PLACE!" Natas said, his eyes glowing like burning hot coals.

CHAPTER SIX

The three stared in terror. Their minds were in a whirl, thinking this couldn't be true.

Natas stretched out his hand, and a cigar materialized in it. He put the cigar in his mouth, reached out his hand, flipped his index finger, and a flame flared up on his fingertip. He lit the cigar and enjoyed several puffs as he watched the three frightened men.

"Now I get it. Natas spelled backwards is Satan!" Sharpy stammered, starring wide-eyed.

"That's right, <u>SATAN</u> in person. I wondered just how long it would take you guys to figure out who I am and where you are."

The three men were speechless and could only stare with wide-open eyes.

"Now that you've got it all figured out and know where you are, I'll let you in on a little secret. You three are my prize catch," Satan boasted with pride as he puffed contentedly on his cigar.

Again fear struck their hearts at the thought of being trapped like animals.

"Just calm down and relax," Satan said, enjoying another drag on his cigar and lazily blowing a smoke ring. "You boys should try one of these cigars; they're my favorite brand. They won't hurt you; I've been smoking them for thousands of years."

"I'll try one," Birdy volunteered, regaining some of his composure. "I'll try anything once."

"That's my boy, just reach up and pluck one out of the air for yourself," Satan instructed.

Birdy reached up, as if picking something out of the air, and a cigar appeared between his thumb and fingers.

"This is pretty neat," Birdy said happily, waving the cigar at his two friends. "Now if you'll do that finger thing again, I'll light this stogy and try it."

Satan flipped his forefinger and it caught fire. Birdy leaned over, stuck the tip of his cigar in the flame, and started puffing. After it was lit, he straightened up and took a long, deep drag on the cigar. Immediately he started gagging, coughing, and gasping for air.

"What kind of cigars <u>are</u> these?" Birdy sputtered through gasps for air.

"They're my special premium brand. My favorite cigar," Satan proudly stated, blowing another smoke ring.

"They may be a premium brand, but they taste like horse manure to me!" Birdy gasped, throwing the cigar down and stomping it.

"That's no way to treat a fine cigar," Satan said, taking another puff on his cigar.

"This can't be true," B.G. mumbled to himself.

"This place sucks!" Sharpy complained. "We've got to get out of here...somehow."

"I think we got diddled by the green finger of fate," Birdy said, regaining his breath.

"We've just got to get out of here! Is there some way to get out of this damned hellhole?" B.G. asked Satan.

"There may be," Satan said, puffing on his cigar and calmly flicking off the ashes. "That is, if you're sure you want out."

"Yes, yes. We'll do anything to get out of here," Sharpy pleaded.

"It is possible, but very difficult," Satan mused.

"We'll take it!" B.G. quickly answered. "We don't care how difficult it is, we want out. This place is driving us crazy."

"What do we have to do to get out of here?" Sharpy asked eagerly.

"Go back to earth and get people to come here," Satan replied with a smile and a puff on his cigar.

"I ain't going to get people to come here!" Birdy stated flatly.

"Then you can stay here with me while your friends go back to earth."

"Oh, no, no, no. I'll go," Birdy blurted out, afraid at the thought of remaining there with the devil any longer.

"No one will want to come down here when we tell them what this place is like!" Sharpy argued.

"Then don't tell them. Let it be a big surprise," Satan said with a sly smile. "They can enjoy everything they want for as long as they desire."

"We know!" B.G. quipped sourly. "How are we going to get people to come here?"

"All you have to do is get people to live the way you three lived, and they'll end up here," Satan said glowingly.

"That sounds easy enough, seeing as how we had a lot of practice at it," Sharpy stated with a smile.

"It may not be as easy as you think," Satan cautioned.

"Let's go!" B.G. said, grabbing his two partners.

"Hold it!" Satan ordered. "First, you have to learn the rules and understand the credits and points you need to earn your way out of here."

"I knew there had to be some catch. You don't get something for nothing, not even down here," Birdy grumbled.

"If you violate any of the rules, or do a good deed, your record will be wiped clean and you'll have to start all over again," Satan warned.

"Looks like we could lose points as fast as we can make them," grumbled Birdy.

"Has anyone ever made it out of here and stayed out?" B.G. anxiously asked.

"Only one so far, but he may not be able to stay out. It's beginning to look like I may get him back," Satan said with an amusing smile.

"That doesn't matter because we're getting out of here and staying out!" B.G. stated with finality.

"I think we're getting into a fixed game," Birdy murmured to his two friends.

"The second rule is, you can't take a life."

"That sucks!" B.G. angrily stated and clutching his fists. "Because I sure would like to stick it to old Valletta for sending us to this happy hunting ground."

"When one of you reaches one hundred points, you'll be set free. Credits are given for minor offenses, and it takes one hundred credits to equal one point," Satan continued, putting out his cigar in the palm of his hand.

"Just how are we to earn these credits and points?" B.G. asked.

"Are you guys familiar with a book called the Bible?"

"I saw one once," Birdy stated.

"I've heard of it," Sharpy said.

"I think I ordered a subscription to it once," replied B.G. with a smile.

"It's a do-gooder book full of "thou shall nots" from beginning to end. Better yet, I'll show you," Satan said.

With a wave of his hand, a giant screen appears, showing the Ten Commandments and other offenses. The screen scrolled through hundreds and hundreds of misdeeds, with their credit and point values:

No other Gods before me	25 points
Fornication	5 points
Forgetting the Sabbath	75 credits
Murder	10 points
Drug addiction	36 credits
Alcohol addiction	17 credits
Prostitution	12 points
Coveting	25 credits
Concealing evidence	4 points
Spousal abuse	15 points
Child abuse	15 points
Animal abuse	15 points
Incest	10 points
Rape	12 points
Fraud	30 credits
Swearing	15 credits
Polluting	10 points
Cheating	5 points
Lying	40 credits
Destroying a marriage	15 points

| Destroying love | 15 points |
| Hatred | 7 points |

The screen continued to quickly scroll through an endless number of offenses with their values in credits and points.

"We can't memorize all that stuff!" Birdy stammered in amazement.

"You don't have to remember it, "Satan stated, tearing off a very long sheet of paper from the computer's printer, folding it, and handing it to them. "Look this over; you'll get full credit for whatever you do, so don't worry".

The three unfolded the long sheet of misdeeds and looked at it in astonishment.

"Here is the big prize. If you can get a person to lose his soul, you'll get the maximum of one hundred points and be out of here immediately."

"Just how are we supposed to do that?" B.G. cried, exasperated with the whole thing.

"Work on everyone, especially those Christians," Satan said with a fiendish smile. His red eyes started to glow brighter and brighter. "Each time he does something that is unchristian, reward him with success and money. He'll soon learn what to do. Then I'll have him!"

"No wonder money is supposed to be the root of all evil," Sharpy murmured, as if thinking out loud.

"That sounds too hard," Birdy complained.

"It's not difficult because people backslide every day. But remember, no good deeds, no violating the rules, and no funny stuff! You're there on business, not to have fun," Satan warned the three.

B. G had been deep in thought, pondering many questions. Then he spoke, "It's beginning to sound like we could lose points faster than we can make them."

"I said it wouldn't be easy," Satan reiterated. "But that's the only way you're going to get out of here. Take it or leave it."

"We'll take it," B.G. grumbled. "How can we get a lot of points fast?"

"Kill someone," Satan said calmly.

"You said we couldn't take a life!" Sharpy pointed out quickly. "Just how are we to do that?"

"It's easy," Satan calmly said. "Get someone else to do it for you by using his anger, greed, hatred, or jealousy. Any of these emotions are good for inciting someone to murder. If you use them just right, you can break up marriages and friendships too."

Birdy was still trying to figure out the points and credits. "Explain that part again about the credits; I don't get it."

"Credits are given for minor misdeeds that are not quite good enough to be considered as points," Satan replied.

"How is that?" asked Sharpy.

"A little white lie may be worth no more than a tenth of a credit, whereas a lie may be worth forty credits, more or less."

"That makes it clear as mud," grumbled Birdy.

"If you want a lot of points fast, I'd suggest going to a football game," Satan stated, not disturbed by Birdy's remark. "You'll have many fans there to work on. Getting fans drunk during the game would be worth five credits for each of you. If you can get them fighting, it may be worth as much as two points each."

"Stop it! Stop it! No more!" B.G. shouted, covering his ears with his hands. "This is getting more complicated and confusing by the minute. We're going to need a score keeper to keep track of all this stuff!"

"Don't worry about that," reassured Satan, lighting up another cigar. "I'll be keeping score."

Birdy leaned over to Sharpy and whispered, "I don't think we're going to like his scorekeeping."

"I'll bet he cheats. That's why only one person has made it out of here so far," Sharpy replied softly.

"I'll be watching everything you do on this screen," Satan warned. With a wave of his hand the screen lit up showing a giant TV screen with a football game already in progress.

"How will we know if we're allowed to do something, and how many points its worth?" Sharpy asked.

"You can summon me any time you want by saying my name and asking. Now, while you're on earth, you'll be able to see each other, but no one else will be able to see you. If you want someone to see you, just think it, and they will be able to see you briefly. A word of caution about talking. Don't talk too loud, or people will hear you. You will be heard as faint voices. If you want people to hear you, shout and they will hear you loud and clear."

"Boy! I can scare the devil out of people with that one," Birdy blurted with a smile, rubbing his hands together in anticipation.

"That wasn't what I had in mind, Birdy!" Satan said, looking displeased. "You'll also be able to hear what people are thinking."

"That's great!" exclaimed Sharpy. "I always wanted to know what some of those women were thinking."

Satan gave Sharpy a disgusted look but continued his instructions. "You'll be able to move objects around, or jab a horse in the ass so he bucks his rider off. This is always good for a whole string of swear words. Some of those cowboys have swearing down to a fine science."

"This is sounding better all the time," B.G. happily stated. "What else can we do?"

"You will have other powers not common to mortals. You can appear instantly anyplace you desire, and you can soar through the air like a bird."

"Wow! I can fly through the air with my pigeons," Birdy said wistfully.

"You'll probably scare the hell out of them if you try that," B.G. stated, laughing.

"You'll be able to create illusions," Satan added.

"What kind of illusions?" Birdy asked with great interest.

"Make people see things that are not there, and things they do see you can make disappear or change into something else. Also, you can make people hear anything you want them to hear, like horns or whistles."

"This sounds like it could be fun, fun, fun come Halloween," Birdy said with a mischievous smile.

"Whatever you want to create, just think about it and wave your hand or wiggle your fingers. For example, you can make an invisible force field just by thinking about it and waving your hand or wiggling your fingers. However, a force field will last only for a few seconds, so you have to make good use of it while it lasts."

Sharpy looked at the TV screen and shouted, "Hey, you guys, look at this! The Falcons are playing the Mustangs. I always wanted to get even with those damned Falcons for losing me so much money on their lousy games. Oh, sweet revenge. Let's go!"

"Hold it!" Satan commanded. "I can see right now I'm going to have trouble with you three. You're not there for fun and games. You had all your fun and games down here. You're there strictly for business—to make points and nothing else! If I catch you using your powers just for fun, I'll jerk your ass back here so fast your shoes will be standing there smoking, and you'll lose everything you've earned. Is that clear?"

"Yes, sir," B.G. and Sharpy replied in unison.

"But we couldn't help it if it turned out funny," Birdy softly suggested.

"To help you develop all your powers and skills, instead of relying on just one or two, I've put a limit on their use. You can use a particular power or skill only once every hour."

"Can we use our abilities to screw up the football game and make the players fight?" B.G. asked.

"Oh, yes, by all means. Not only the players, but also the fans and coaches as well. Get everyone fighting and swearing. The more fighting and swearing, the more points you'll get," Satan said with a delighted smile.

"What are we waiting for?" B.G. said with a broad grin. "It looks like the game has already started."

"Yeah! I can hardly wait. The Falcons are going to get a screw job they'll never forget," Sharpy threatened. "Look out, Falcons, here we come!"

CHAPTER SEVEN

The stadium was filled with cheering fans, drinking and rooting for their favorite team. The three devils advocates materialized in one aisle of the immense stadium, near the television broadcast booth. The game was being broadcast on national television. At first, they were a little surprised at the quick change in their surroundings and just stood there looking around.

"I think they can see us," Birdy anxiously claimed, looking at the fans around him.

"No they can't," Sharpy insisted. "They're just watching the game."

Still unsure, Birdy floated over and stood in front of two fans. He waved his hand in their faces, but they took no notice of him and continued watching the game. He bent over close to one spectator's face and made silly faces at him; nothing happened. The fan kept on drinking his beer and shouting for the Falcons. Satisfied that he was invisible, Birdy floated back to his friends.

"You're right, they can't see me. I tried everything to get his attention and couldn't," Birdy stated.

"How about stirring up a little mischief?" B.G. asked. "You guys watch me. I'm going to get something started—we can't make any points just standing here."

"Just remember: Satan is watching, so no funny business," Sharpy cautioned the other two.

"Don't worry! I'm not going to have fun. I'm just going to cause a little trouble between those two guys up there near the top," B.G. stated, pointing to two spectators named Buddy and Dave.

Buddy and Dave were two ardent football fans. They were totally engrossed in the game, and also enjoying their beer. So far, each had consumed several beers and both were feeling no pain. B.G. floated up to an empty seat and sat down behind the two men. He reached down and pinched Buddy on the butt. Buddy got a surprised look on his face and stared at Dave, the stranger sitting next to him. Dave was busy shaking his fist at the players and drinking between shouts. But he turned in his seat when he noticed Buddy staring at him.

"What's your problem?" Dave asked, his tongue uncooperative.

"Nothing," replied Buddy.

"Then keep it that way," Dave stammered.

Buddy decided it would be best to ignore the stranger, so he resumed his interest in the game and drinking. This time B.G. reached down and patted Buddy on the butt with good, firm pats. Buddy suspicious, jerked his head around and gave Dave a dirty look.

"Hey, you!" Buddy snapped. "Cut out the funny business!"

Dave looked around at Buddy, but not knowing what Buddy was talking about he paid little attention to what Buddy had said. Then he resumed watching the game. This time B.G. gave both of Buddy's cheeks a good, hard squeeze.

Buddy jumped to his feet and shouted, "All right! That does it, you fruitcake. One more time and I'll flatten that big nose of yours."

"What the hell are you talking about?" Dave growled, puzzled at the drunken stranger next to him.

"You know what!" Buddy snapped. "You keep grabbing my ass."

"Not me. I'm busy watching the game. If you've got problems, go play with yourself!" Dave said, becoming angry at the accusations.

"Oh, no," Buddy stated, not believing him.

"You're either drunk and imagining things or you're nuts."

"You don't see anyone sitting behind us, do you?" Buddy slurred.

Dave looked around and saw nothing but empty seats.

"No, I can't see anyone. So what?"

"Then keep your damned hands to yourself, or I'll kick your ass," warned Buddy.

The two fans settled down to cheering for their respective teams and consuming more beer. Everything was quiet for a while. Then B.G. went to work on Dave by pinching him hard on the butt.

"Ouch!" Dave yelled, jumping to his feet and shouting at Buddy, "Now who's playing games?"

"Shut up and sit down; I didn't touch you," Buddy said.

"You pinched my ass," Dave snarled.

"Ah, shut up and sit down. Drink your beer and quit imagining things," Buddy grumbled.

The two let their tempers cool off, and Dave sat back down. B.G. giggled to himself; then he reached down and firmly patted both men on the butt. Both men jumped to their feet, with tempers flaring.

"All right, you flaky son of a bitch! Maybe this will cool off your hot passion," Buddy shouted, dumping his cup of beer on Dave's head.

"You bastard! Nobody does that to me and gets away with it!" yelled Dave, wiping beer out of his eyes.

"Says who?" Buddy mocked.

"Says me!" Dave snarled, letting go with a hard right cross to Buddy's chin, knocking him down.

"That does it!" snapped Buddy, staggering to his feet.

The fight was on! Fists and feet went flying as the two slugged it out. They were down in the aisle when O'Malley, the stadium policeman, came running to break up the fight. O'Malley was a giant of a man with a short temper and a passion for fighting. He bent down and grabbed the two men by their collars.

"Break it up!" O'Malley shouted.

"Break it up before me Irish temper gets the best of me and I flatten ye both with me nightstick."

O'Malley had the men by the collars when he pulled them apart. Roughly he lifted them to their feet. Even though O'Malley was holding on to their collars, they still took wild swings at each other.

"Stop it!" O'Malley growled, shaking the two by their collars. "Now what's this ruckus about?"

"This fruitcake keeps pinching my ass and won't leave me alone," Buddy blurted.

"Bullshit, you lying son of a bitch! You keep making passes at me," Dave snarled.

Buddy took a swing at Dave, but O'Malley caught his fist in midair with his big hand and started squeezing it hard. The pain showed on Buddy's face and O'Malley let go.

"Now hold it, laddies. If there's goin' to be any fightin', it's me that'll do the fightin', understand?" O'Malley warned in his Irish brogue. "Now stand still on each side of me until me gets this thing sorted out, and <u>no funny business!</u>"

The two stood on each side of O'Malley facing each other, their intense anger branded on their faces. B.G. reached down and grabbed both of O'Malley's buns and gave them a good squeeze. O'Malley's temper exploded as he jumped back from the two men.

"Ye both are fruitcakes!" he shouted. "I'm arrestin' ye both for assaultin' an officer, disturbin' the peace, and anythin' else me thinks of."

O'Malley roughly snapped handcuffs on the two and began pushing and shoving them down the aisle toward the exit.

B.G., Birdy, and Sharpy were laughing and wiping tears from their eyes as they watched O'Malley march the two men out of the stadium.

"That was really funny, B.G.," Birdy said, wiping another tear from his cheek.

"I wonder what old Satan would have to say about that little performance," B.G. said, trying to control his laughter. "I sure got them mad and fighting!"

"He said we could summon him any time we wanted. So let's ask him," Sharpy suggested.

B.G. leaned over as if speaking to the floor, "Hey, Satan old boy, we need you."

Satan immediately appeared before the three with a look of disapproval on his face.

"Well, what do you think of that performance? Do we get a lot of points?" B.G. happily asked.

"It looked to me like you were having more fun than anything else, even though you did get them fighting and swearing," Satan stated flatly.

"Now wait just a doggoned minute. It just happened to turn out funny. I <u>did</u> get them fighting and swearing," B.G. angrily stated.

"Well, that may be worth two credits. I'll have to think about it," Satan said coolly.

"Only two lousy credits? At this rate we're never going to get a hundred points," B.G. complained.

"I think you just got diddled with the green finger," Birdy whispered.

"If you're going to call the shots like that, then you'd better keep your eyes on this game. We're going to screw up this game like you've never seen a game screwed up before," B.G. angrily snapped.

With that Satan smiled, gave a small salute, and vanished.

"Would you look at that," Sharpy said, pointing to the Scoreboard. "The Falcons are ahead seven to nothing! We have to do something about that. You guys want to help me readjust the score? I can hardy wait to get even with those damned Falcons."

"Sure, we'll help," Birdy replied. "I've got a good idea for Melrose, that big right end for the Falcons."

The players were lined up on the scrimmage line, and the Falcon quarterback was calling out signals. Birdy glided down onto the field and slipped up behind Melrose. He wiggled his fingers at Melrose's shoes and the shoelaces came untied. When the ball was snapped, Melrose lunged forward, stumbled, and almost fell. He sat down and carefully tied his shoelaces to make sure they were tight.

The two teams got back on the scrimmage line, and Elrod, the Falcon quarterback, started calling signals as he looked right and left, checking the line. Birdy glided up behind Melrose again and wiggled his fingers. This time the shoelaces not only came untied, but they pulled part way out of the shoes. When the ball was snapped, Melrose leaped forward and went sprawling when his foot came out of his shoe.

"Damn it! "Melrose snorted. "I can't understand why these sons of bitches won't stay tied."

Getting up, he hobbled over to his shoe, sat down, pulled it on, and tied the laces in several knots.

"Hey, B.G., look at Melrose. I'm starting to get his dander up. He's going to get me a lot of points before I'm through with him," Birdy gleefully stated.

The down marker showed the third down was coming up. The players got set, and Elrod started calling signals as he looked the line over again.

"Hey, Birdy, watch this," Sharpy shouted.

"Sharpy slipped up behind Melrose and gave him a hard, swift kick, sending him offside. The referees immediately started blowing their whistles and throwing flags. One referee ran up, grabbed the ball, and paced off a five-yard penalty against the Falcons.

"Damn it! I didn't jump offside," Melrose complained to Elrod. "Someone kicked me in the ass and <u>knocked</u> me offsides. Somebody keeps messin' around back here, and I'm gettin' pissed."

Elrod could not figure out what he was talking about and just shrugged his shoulders. The two teams reassembled on the scrimmage line and settled down to play. The ball was snapped. Elrod tried a long pass, but it comes up incomplete. The Falcons were forced to kick on their fourth down.

The teams got set for the kick, the ball was snapped, and the ball was kicked high. B.G. held out his hand and waved the ball over to a Mustang player's hands. The player ran the ball up to the fifty-yard line before being brought down. The Mustangs' first two downs resulted in incomplete passes. On the third down the pass was completed, and the ball was run in for a touchdown. This made the score seven to six in favor of the Falcons. The players got set for the extra point, the ball was snapped, and the kick was good. The game was tied, and the fans began cheering for a good, close game.

The Mustang kicker sent the ball high and deep into Falcon territory. The ball was coming down straight toward Dunn, the fullback, when Birdy jerked Dunn's hand up in the air, signaling for a fair catch. Not seeing the signal, the Mustang players smeared Dunn just as he caught the ball. Shagla, the Falcon's defensive-team quarterback, ran over to Dunn and helped him to his feet.

"What's the matter with you, signaling for a fair catch on a kickoff?" Shagla demanded.

"That wasn't me," Dunn replied. "Something or someone grabbed my hand and jerked it up in the air and held it there!"

"Well, I didn't see anything," grumbled Shagla, wondering what his teammate was talking about.

The referee scooped up the ball and spotted it on the Falcon's twenty-yard line.

"Have either of you thought about using your force field yet?" B.G. asked.

"Haven't had a chance," replied Sharpy.

"Me neither," Birdy added.

"Well then, just stand back and watch this next play," B.G. stated with an impish grin.

The Falcons had a quick huddle to discuss new tactics; then they spread out on the scrimmage line. Elrod started calling signals and checking the line right and left. The ball was snapped to Elrod and he started drifting back, looking for a receiver, when he spotted Knight, the right end, in the open. He fired the ball straight down the field to Knight, who leaped into the air and caught it perfectly. Knight tucked the ball in tight and, with no tacklers close by, he was headed for a touchdown.

"Here goes that force field we're supposed to have," B.G. said, stretching out his arms and wiggling his fingers.

Knight was running at full speed when he hit the invisible wall. He bounced off the wall, lost the ball, and fell to the ground with the wind knocked out of him. The ball went bouncing along on the ground until a Mustang player fell on it at the thirty-six-yard line. While the Mustang players were trying to get back on the line, B.G., Sharpy, and Birdy ran around tripping the Falcon players so they had trouble getting back to the scrimmage line.

The television broadcasters were making comments about the game as the television cameras showed the Scoreboard.

"It looks like the Falcon team is having trouble standing up," the first announcer quipped, lifting his binoculars to his eyes.

"I've seen players trip before, but this is the first time I've seen a whole team falling over their own feet," the second announcer commented.

Eventually everyone got back on the line. The ball was snapped and thrown to Jones, a Mustang receiver, who managed to catch it. Two Falcon players rushed in to tackle Jones, but they were tripped before they could get a hand on him. With the field clear, Jones ran the ball all the way into the end zone for a quick touchdown. The fans were wildly cheering, and loving the new turn of events.

On the kickoff, the Mustang kicker sent the ball high and downfield. The Mustangs rushed down the field and stopped the Falcons on the forty-one-yard line. This brought out the Falcon offensive team.

The teams got set on the scrimmage line and the ball was snapped to Elrod. He started dropping back, looking for an open receiver, but before he could get rid of the ball, he was hit hard from behind and it slipped out of his hands. A Mustang fell on the bouncing ball at the thirty-yard line. While the players were walking up to the line, Birdy slipped up behind Melrose and untied both his shoes. Melrose almost stepped out of them. Noticing his shoes untied again, he lost his temper.

"Damn these son of a bitches!" he yelled as he plunked himself down to tie his shoes again. "You damned clodhoppers will stay tied this time."

He carefully tied the shoelaces in square knots, then wrapped the laces around his ankles and tied them in double square knots.

"That'll hold you mothers!" he angrily growled, inspecting his handiwork before getting up to continue the game.

Birdy was not to be outsmarted by his fancy knot tying. He waited until the players were on the scrimmage line, then wiggled his fingers, first at Melrose's shoe and then at Walker's shoe. Wiggling his fingers again, he tied both players' shoelaces together. The ball was snapped and both players charged forward, only to trip and fall to the ground. This, of course, left a big hole in the line. The Mustangs took full advantage of it and ran the ball down to the seventeen-yard line before the Falcon's Brickhouse brought the ball carrier down.

"Who the hell is screwing around with my shoes?" Melrose snapped at Walker.

"Not me," Walker replied perplexed.

The two managed to untangle their shoes, then each player retied his shoes. They double-checked to make sure the knots were tight. Melrose got up and went storming over to their halfback, Brubaker.

"First, someone keeps untying my shoes and kicking me in the ass, sending me offside," Melrose growled. "Have you seen anyone back here messin' around with my shoes?"

"Ain't seen anyone," Brubaker replied, looking at Melrose and wondering if he had been hit in the head too many times.

"If you see anyone back here messin' around with my shoes, let me know 'cause I'm goin' to kick his ass so hard he'll have to take his hat off to fart!"

"Yeah, I'll keep a lookout and let you know if I see anyone," Brubaker answered, still puzzled at what Melrose was talking about.

The referee spotted the ball on the Falcons' seventeen-yard line as the Mustangs went into a huddle.

The Mustang quarterback, Thompson, was encouraging his team: "Okay, guys. The Falcons are having a streak of bad luck right now, so let's make the most of it and get another touchdown before half time. Give it all you've got. Play 34-X. Break!"

The huddle broke. The players hustled up to the scrimmage line and got set. Thompson called out signals as he looked right and left, checking the line. The ball was snapped to Thompson and he started drifting back, looking for his receivers, Lepold and Jones. Lepold started cutting across to the center of the field, and it looked like he might be in the clear. Thompson cocked his arm and fired the ball towards the spot where Lepold should be when the ball arrived. Lepold was running flat out, along with a Falcon player. It looked like the Falcon player could intercept the ball.

"Oh no you don't!" Birdy snapped, seeing what was about to happen.

He wiggled his fingers at the ball and it made a great, sweeping curve to the other side of the field into the hands of Jones. Jones caught the ball, tucked it in, stiff-armed a would-be tackier, and ran the ball in for the touchdown.

"I'm flabbergasted," the first announcer said. "I don't believe what I think I just saw. Thompson just threw a big curve in football! That's impossible! We'll have to watch the instant replay to see if it actually happened."

The instant replay was run; it showed Thompson throwing the curve.

"There you have it, folks, a curve thrown in football," the first announcer said, scratching his head. "I wouldn't have believed it if I hadn't seen it with my own eyes—twice."

The head referee was standing with his mouth gaped open and blinking his eyes. "Did you see what I think I just saw, or am I hallucinating?"

"I don't think I saw it either. Maybe we're having the same hallucination," the second referee said, rubbing his eyes.

The players got set to kick for the extra point. The ball was snapped...set...and the kick was good. The numbers on the Scoreboard changed to show the Mustangs with twenty-one points and the Falcons with seven.

On the kickoff, the Mustangs made a good kick, sending the ball downfield to the twenty-yard line. A Falcon player caught the ball and ran it back up to the forty-six-yard line before he was stopped. After two downs, the Falcons had not made any gain and still had ten yards to go for a first down. The players got set on the line for the third down. Elrod called the signals as he checked the line. The ball was snapped to Elrod and he started backing up, looking for a receiver. Norris, the left end, was wide open. Elrod was getting set to throw to Norris when Sharpy ran up behind him. Just as Elrod cocked his arm to throw, Sharpy hit the ball hard with his fist, sending the ball backward ten yards. It looked like Elrod had made a backward pass. Kersey fell on the ball and recovered it for the Falcons.

"It looks like the Falcons are having trouble knowing which way to throw the ball," the first announcer said with a chuckle.

"It sure looked that way," the second announcer agreed.

The Falcons were out of downs and were forced to kick on there forth down. The ball was snapped and the kicker made a good punt, sending the ball flying down the field. One of the Mustangs caught the ball and ran it back near the forty-second yard line before Gilmore brought the ball carrier down.

"Hey, B.G., aren't we supposed to be the devil's advocates?" Sharpy asked.

"Well, yes, I guess so. Why?" he asked.

"Satan has a pitchfork. So why can't we have one?" Sharpy asked.

"Yeah," mused B.G., smiling and considering the possibilities. "We could prod up some real live action with some of those babies."

"I'll ask him if we can have some. Satan! How about giving us some pitchforks," Sharpy yelled at the ground, with his hand cupped around his mouth.

Immediately three red hot pitchforks appeared on the ground in front of the three.

Birdy leaned over and picked up one of the pitchforks but quickly dropped it. "Ouch! Damn they're hot!"

"Well, what did you expect? They're direct from the manufacturer," Sharpy stated.

They gingerly picked up the pitchforks and looked them over, switching them back and forth between hands until the pitchforks cooled off enough for them to handle.

"A couple of jabs with this baby and I'll bet a player could move real fast," B.G. stated with a crafty grin, as he touched the tips of the tines.

"Yeah, a jab in the ass with a hot pitchfork should make any player real hard to catch," Birdy muttered.

"You guys watch this. I'm going to have some fun with Jonas," B.G. said with a chuckle.

He drifted up to the players set on the line and stopped behind Jonas, a Falcon lineman. He stuck the hot pitchfork up to Jones' crotch, making him yell and jump offside.

"Ouch! Ouch! Ouch! Who's tryin' to burn up my business?" Jonas yelled, dancing around and holding his crotch.

The referees' whistles blew, and flags were thrown all over the place. The referee paced off a five-yard penalty against the Falcons and placed the ball on the forty-seven yard line.

"You guys keep your eyes glued on the line. I'm going to try out one of my new powers," Sharpy said with great flair.

Sharpy wiggled his fingers at the Mustang linemen, turning them into ferocious, roaring lions ready to attack the Falcon linemen. The Falcons were so shocked they froze in place and made no effort to move when the ball was snapped.

Thompson noticed the linemen not moving and took full advantage of the situation to make an end run. He would have gone all the way and made a touchdown if it had not been for Birdy's pitchfork accidentally getting in the way and tripping him. He went sprawling to the ground and lost the ball, which was recovered by a Falcon.

The Falcons had the ball on their own thirty-four-yard line. The players got set and the ball was snapped to Elrod. He tried a quick, short pass that was incomplete. When the players got set, Birdy untied Melrose's shoe again. When the ball was snapped, Sharpy knocked the ball out of Elrod's hands, and there was a mad scramble for it.

In the scramble, Melrose's shoe got knocked off and it flew up in the air. Birdy, concentrating on the airborne shoe, wiggled his fingers, making the players see it as the football. Paxton, for the Falcons, caught the shoe and tore down the field to make a touchdown, with all the players following in hot pursuit. Paxton crossed the goal line holding the shoe high over his head. After he paraded around with the "football" held high, it slowly started changing back into Melrose's shoe. Paxton, seeing he had a shoe in his hand, spiked it on the ground in disgust.

While the players were running up the field chasing Paxton with the shoe the referees were standing with their mouths open and scratching their heads.

"Where the hell is everybody going? The damned ball is right here in front of us!" the head referee said in disgust.

"This is the screwiest game I ever refereed," the assistant referee complained.

"I must be getting ready for the rubber room," the head referee mumbled.

At the television broadcast booth, the announcers were laughing so hard tears came to their eyes, and they could hardly talk.

"I think I've...ha ha...seen...ha ha...about everything now! Paxton just made a...touchdown with a shoe...ha ha ha! It looks like this game is turning into a circus...ha ha...and the fans are loving it!" the announcer managed to say.

The down marker showed the third down was coming up. The Falcons tried to run the play, but they were stopped at the line of scrimmage. With their fourth and last down coming up, they were forced to kick. The Falcon kicker sent the ball high, and a Mustang caught it on his own thirty-yard line. On the first play, the Mustangs completed a long pass and ran the ball in for a touchdown. The kick for the extra point was no good because the kicker sent the ball wide, missing the uprights.

The first half of the game ended with the Scoreboard showing the Mustangs with twenty-seven points and the Falcons with seven points. As the Falcons left the field for the locker room, they were silent except for Elrod and Brubaker.

"I'm not anxious to hear what Mitch is going to say once he gets us in the locker room," Elrod admitted.

"You're not the only one. He's going to be mad, and when he's mad, he's mad all over and turns into a thirty-two-tooth reaming machine," Brubaker added.

"We're sure going to get reamed good this time," Elrod stated.

Mitch, the Falcons' head coach, and Colter, his assistant, were walking along together as they followed the team, heading to the locker room.

"Lou sure is going to have my butt in a sling over this game," Mitch confessed.

"It won't be just yours. The whole staff will be fired," Colter stated glumly.

"He wants his team to make it to the play-offs so bad he can taste it," Mitch admitted.

"Judging by the looks of it, it would take nothing short of a miracle to pull this game out of the fire," Colter stated frankly.

Nothing was said as the players entered the locker room and sat down. No one was talking, and the only sounds were those of the players shuffling into the locker room and plunking themselves down. When Mitch and Colter entered the room, everything fell deathly still. Mitch paced up and down in front of the players with his fists resting on his hips. The fire in his eyes was plain to see, and the players wouldn't even take a quick glance at him. He paused only long enough to look the team over; then he started pacing back and forth again, glaring at the team.

"In all my thirty years of coaching, I've never seen a more screwed-up game than this one," Mitch ranted. "Just what the hell do you guys think you're doing out there, putting on a comedy show? Well, you're doing a damned good job of it because the fans are laughing themselves silly! If they laugh any harder, they'll have to be carried out on stretchers!"

By now, Mitch's voice had reached a high crescendo, and the veins on his neck were standing out. He was not letting any player escape his fiery scrutiny.

"This game is going down in the record books! Do you know why? I'll tell you why! We'll be the only team in history to make a touchdown with a shoe! And Shagla, you can't signal for a fair catch on a kick off!"

Mitch continued pacing up and down in front of the players. He paused as if thinking, then turned his attention to individual team members.

"Melrose! Don't you know how to tie your shoes yet? Do I have to tie them for you? And for goodness' sake, don't tie your shoes to Walker's!"

After a brief pause to let his blood pressure lower, Mitch started tongue-lashing the players again.

"Elrod...try to remember, in this game you throw the damned ball forward not backward!" Mitch yelled.

Mitch shook his head and muttered to himself as he paced. "Some quarterback, doesn't know which way to throw the damned ball. It's sure a hell of a time for Leonard, my star quarterback, to be in the hospital undergoing surgery."

After a long pause, Paxton spoke up in his own defense, trying to justify his actions: "Coach, it was a football when I caught it."

"Sure it was! And somehow it miraculously changed into a shoe after you made the touchdown!" Mitch snorted, not believing a word of it. "Well in that case, you must need glasses. So the first thing tomorrow morning, I want Doc to examine your eyes. In fact, I want the whole damned team's eyes checked!"

All the players hung their heads, looking at the floor. None of them want to look Mitch straight in the eyes for fear he would start on them.

"You guys don't really expect me to believe the Mustang's whole defensive line turned into roaring lions right before your eyes!" Mitch snapped.

"They did, and someone kicked me in the ass, making me jump off-side," Melrose protested.

"Someone tried to burn up my business, making <u>me</u> jump offside," Jonas said.

"Yeah! and someone held my hand up for a fair catch on the kick off," Shagla added.

"Just who the hell do you guys think you're kidding? I wasn't born yesterday!" Mitch growled.

"But, Mitch, there's something strange going on out there. Guys just don't trip over nothing, run into invisible walls, or catch a shoe if something strange isn't going on," Elrod stated in defense of the whole team.

Mitch started pacing up and down in front of the team again, deep in thought. After some time, he stopped and faced them.

"I'll say something strange is going on. You guys are ready for the funny farm, or you're all hallucinating. <u>That's</u> what's going on!" Mitch stated angrily.

Then he paused for a few moments, thinking. He ran his finger up and down the line of men, pointing to each player in turn as he started pacing again.

"Have you guys been smoking some of the wacky Mexican weed or sniffing some funny dust?" Mitch asked each player. Well, if you have, please tell old Mitch, so I'll at least know <u>what the hell is going</u> on!" Mitch yelled.

All the players kept looking at the floor as they shook their heads from side to side in answer to his question.

"Well, then…if you're clean it must be something else that would cause the whole damned team to hallucinate," Mitch said, starting to regain some of his composure.

He continued pacing back and forth, trying to figure out what would cause the whole team to go crazy. He finally hit upon an idea.

"Maybe it's the water. You're so used to drinking putrid, chlorinated city water you can't handle the good pure spring water we brought with us. Well, if that's your trouble, from now on you'll drink this damned, stinking city water. Maybe that'll clear your heads!" he growled.

Mitch looked at Paulson, one of his assistants, and paused to think for a moment before he spoke.

"Paulson, empty the barrels of spring water we brought with us and fill them with this stinking city water," Mitch instructed.

Turning his attention back to the team, Mitch warned, "I'll tell you guys one thing, if you don't get your act together this second half of the game, the Mustangs are going to stomp a mud hole in your ass and kick it dry!"

After he finished reaming out the team and jacking them up a few notches, he went over to Colter and sat down. He needed time to unwind, time to allow his blood pressure to return to normal.

"That was some pep talk," Colter said with a grin.

"You know something?" Mitch said, letting out a big sigh. "I must be getting too old for this shit."

"Sometimes I think we've both been in this business too long," Colter agreed.

"You know, I can usually figure out what is wrong with a team and correct it, but this damned game has me completely baffled. Maybe I should consider retiring," Mitch admitted.

"If the team doesn't get it together this second half, we won't have to worry about retiring," Colter warned his friend.

CHAPTER EIGHT

During the half time, some of the fans milled around while others watched the half time marching bands on the playing field.

"Where is B.G.?" Birdy asked, looking around, trying to find him.

"He went to the Falcons' dressing room. He wanted to see the Falcons get chewed out," Sharpy answered with a smile. "As for me, I'm going back to our old hometown to see what has happened since we've been gone."

"I think I'll stay here and see what trouble I can cause with some of the fans," Birdy stated. "B.G. said to tell you we are to meet at the fifty-yard line for the start of the second half of the game."

"I'll see you there," Sharpy said as he whisked off.

Birdy floated up through the grandstand, looking the fans over. He noticed a boy sitting by his father, enjoying the exhibition the marching band was putting on as he munched on a bag of popcorn and washed it down with a large cola. Birdy thought children should have some trouble in their lives, so decided to pick on the boy. He took the boy's hand and deliberately poured the drink in the father's lap.

"You clumsy idiot!" the father screeched, jumping to his feet. "You've ruined my new pants! This is the last time I'll bring you to a game!"

The boy's feelings were hurt, and tears soon started flowing down his cheeks as he cried silently. Birdy was very pleased with the hurt feelings he had caused, and also with the boy's father swearing.

"That little bit of trouble should get me a few quick points," Birdy said to himself. "Now, on to bigger and better things, so I can get a lot more points!"

He floated down to the concession stand and spotted two intoxicated brothers, Bill and Ernie, staggering out of the restroom on unsteady legs. Bill was having trouble with his zipper.

"This damned zipper is stuck again and I can't get it up," Bill said to his brother, tugging on the zipper.

"Not again," Ernie moaned.

"Can you get it unstuck?"

By now, the two had staggered out close to where the people were coming and going to the concession stand.

"Okay, I'll see if I can get it unstuck again," Ernie replied.

Ernie knelt down in front of Bill, stuck two fingers in Bill's pants behind the zipper and started working with the zipper. Two pious, old ladies happened to walk by and saw Bill fumbling with the zipper.

"Well! The nerve of some people!" the first lady snorted with contempt.

"And in public, too!" the second lady indignantly chimed in.

The two stunned ladies snubbed Bill and Ernie, stuck their noses in the air, snorted, and stomped off to the ladies' restroom.

"I wonder what put a burr under their saddles," Bill mumbled, trying to turn and watch the ladies.

"If you don't stand still, I'm never going to get this zipper free," Ernie growled.

After the zipper was fixed, Bill and Ernie made their way to the concession stand and ordered two beers which, were served in paper cups. After they were served, the two swayed over to a vacant stand to drink.

Bill set his beer down and fumbled in his inside jacket pocket for his bottle of whiskey. Yanking the bottle out, he poured a healthy shot into his cup, then passed the bottle to Ernie. While Bill was busy stuffing the bottle back in his pocket, Birdy moved his beer to the far end of the stand. Seeing his beer at the other end of the stand, Bill staggered over to get it. His mind just was not functioning too well, so he did not make the connection between where he had set the beer down and where it was now. As he reached for his beer, it moved away from him. He blinked his eyes and stared as the beer glided back and forth. Each time the beer stopped, Bill made a grab for it, but the beer always moved just out of his reach. He grabbed for it with one hand, then the other, then with both hands. The beer circled, moved in and out, around and around, and danced before Bill's amazed eyes. In total exasperation, he quit chasing the beer and made his way over to Ernie.

"Did you see my beer dancing and moving funny-like?" Bill whispered.

"You crazy?"

"I've been trying to catch mine, but it keeps running away from me."

"You've been spiking your beer too heavy," Ernie said, casting a curious eye at him.

"It did move! It went this way and that way, and danced around and around," Bill protested, making hand gestures to show how the beer had moved.

"You're drunk," Ernie said in disgust.

"I ain't either!" Bill protested again. "I'm feeling pretty rosy, but I ain't drunk."

"You're drunk because you're starting to act silly. Even I can tell that," Ernie explained.

"I'll show you, you smart aleck. Just watch this," Bill demanded.

Bill made a couple of quick grabs for his beer, but each time it darted away. Ernie just stared in dismay, watching Bill chase his beer from one end of the stand to the other. When Ernie reached for his beer, it darted out of <u>his</u> reach and startled him. By now, Bill was exhausted from chasing his beer, so he propped himself up against the stand next to Ernie.

"You know," Bill panted. "A guy could die from thirst trying to get a drink from these damned cups."

At that point, both cups started floating in the air above the table as both bleary-eyed men watched with awe-stricken faces. The cups finally stopped floating and settled down on the stand.

"If we're not careful," Ernie stammered, "we'll be seeing green snakes and pink elephants."

Birdy got a fiendish smile on his face and started talking out loud to himself, "Well, now it would be a shame to let a golden opportunity like this pass."

Birdy stretched out his arms and wiggled his fingers. A herd of wild, trumpeting, pink elephants appeared, and the two men were so shocked it registered on their faces. Bill fished the bottle out of his pocket and looked at it.

"I think we must have got hold of some bad booze," Bill stammered, as he slowly looked the bottle over.

"I think you're right.   Get rid of it," Ernie suggested.

Bill staggered over to the trashcan and unscrewed the cap.   He began pouring out the whiskey into the trashcan, but he dropped the bottle when a glowing green snake came slithering out of the bottle.

"YE <u>GAWDS!</u>   We've been drinking out of a bottle with a snake in it," Ernie mumbled, starting to gag and cough.   "I think I'm going to be sick. I'm going home."

"I don't feel so good either," Bill agreed.

Birdy had a good laugh as he watched the two men weave their way toward the exit, hanging on to each other.

"I guess I earned myself a lot of points with those two," Birdy said out loud to himself.

As they had planned, B.G., Sharpy, and Birdy met at the fifty-yard line for the second half of the game.   When Sharpy arrived, he was all excited.

"What's with all the excitement?" B.G. asked.

"While you two clowns were goofing off around here, I went back to our old stomping grounds and paid a visit to Sammy, our old bookie," Sharpy blurted out.

"So you went back home and saw Sammy. <u>Big</u> deal!" B.G. mocked.

"You'll never guess who made a big three-million-dollar bet on the Mustangs, "Sharpy replied, ignoring B.G.'s remarks.

"Some of our old friends," Birdy suggested.

"Hell no!" Sharpy quipped. "None of them have that kind of money. It was Valletta, and he doesn't have that kind of cash either. So he dipped into the syndicate money for the whole wad."

"Now isn't that just too bad," mused B.G. "If the Mustangs lose, there is no way he can pay it back. So guess what the boys will do to poor old Vallette?"

"Yeah, fit him with a pair of cement shorts for a swim in the river, "Birdy said, chuckling.

"That would serve the bastard right for what he did to us, "B.G. said, gloating. "Hey, we've been helping the wrong team. We'd better get busy and make sure the Falcons win this game!"

"What about the Falcons making me lose all those football bets? I want to get even!" Sharpy protested.

"Screw your bets!" B.G. snarled. "We need to make points to get out of this mess. We're helping the Falcons win so we can get Vallette."

"That will be impossible, with the Mustangs so far ahead," Birdy complained.

"We'd damned better make sure the Falcons win," B.G. commanded.

"Maybe you're right," Sharpy conceded. "If we can pull this off, Satan should give each of us a hundred points for Vallette."

By now both teams were lined up for the kickoff. The Mustangs were receiving the ball. The Falcon kicker booted the ball high. Birdy grabbed it and started floating down the field in slow motion. The referee's whistle dropped from his mouth as he stared at the floating ball. He shook his head and vigorously rubbed his eyes. When he looked up again, the ball was still slowly floating down the field. At the two-yard line the ball dropped into the hands of a Mustang player who was immediately smeared by the Falcons.

The Mustangs huddled, and Thompson warned the team, "We're down too deep for safety. So we're going for some long yards. Vaught, get down the right side fast, break left, and then run flat out. I'll overthrow, so get down there fast. Break."

The players broke, hustled up to the line, and got set. Thompson started calling signals and checking the line right and left. The ball was snapped. Vaught rushed down the field, cut left, and then ran straight out as hard as he could go. Thompson threw the ball hard at a spot where Vaught should be when the ball arrived. Brownlee saw the long pass and ran in to intercept it for the Falcons.

With a gleam in his eyes, Sharpy shouted to the other two, "Keep your eyes fixed on Brownlee; he is about to make history!"

Sharpy floated up behind Brownlee with the pitchfork in his hand and stayed right behind him every step of the way, jabbing him in the butt and yelling, "Run, <u>you sucker,</u> run!"

The announcers in the TV booth had the cameras turned on Brownlee racing down the field.

"WOW!" the first announcer exclaimed. "That's the fastest yardage I've ever seen! Brownlee just shot past two would-be tacklers so fast they couldn't even lay a hand on him."

"I didn't know a human could run that fast! That has to be some kind of a record," the second announcer added.

"That must have been some kind of pep talk Mitch gave the team at half-time. I sure would like to know what he said," the third announcer stated with a chuckle.

The team was elated and gave Brownlee high fives and slaps on the back. He was walking next to his teammate Coull when Coull asked, "How did you do it? That's faster than I've ever seen anyone run."

"You'd be fast too if a ghost was chasing you, jabbing you in the ass with a hot pitchfork, and yelling "Run, you sucker, run,'" Brownlee answered, rubbing his butt with both hands.

As the defensive team left the field, Mitch came up with a big smile and slapped Brownlee on the shoulder. "That's the way to do it, my boy! That city water did the trick."

"Coach, "Brownlee said, still rubbing his butt and trying to catch his breath, "It wasn't the water, and if I told you, you wouldn't believe me."

"Whatever it was, just keep on doing it."

"Not on your life! My ass feels like a pin cushion," Brownlee flatly stated. "If I ever see that ghost again, I'm going the other way."

Mitch gave Brownlee a puzzled look, then walked off toward Colter, muttering to himself, "First it was lions; now it's ghosts. God, what's next?"

Mitch sat down next to Colter and mumbled, "Now it's ghosts. Well, if that's what it takes, I hope the whole damned team sees ghosts."

Colter cast a suspicious glance at Mitch and wondered what he was mumbling about. Maybe he had been coaching too long and the games were starting to get to him.

"You haven't got your cap screwed on too tight, shutting off the circulation in your head, have you?" Colter asked.

Mitch gave him a quick glance, not knowing what he was talking about, resumed interest in the game as the players got set to kick for the extra point. The ball was snapped; and the kick was good. The Scoreboard numbers changed to show the Falcons now at fourteen and the Mustangs at twenty-seven. The fans were cheering. They were starting to like the game now that the Falcons had started to come to life and put some excitement back in the game.

The Mustangs were to receive on the kickoff. The kick was a good one; the ball went high and deep into Mustang territory. One of the Mustangs caught the ball and ran it back up to the forty-three-yard line before being stopped. The players got set, the ball was snapped to Thompson, and he started drifting back, looking for a receiver, but he couldn't find one in the open. He ran around the end for a two-yard gain before being brought down. On the second down, Thompson made a quick, short pass to Naccarato for a gain of six yards. The referee picked up the ball and placed it on the Falcon's forty-nine-yard line.

"Hey, guys, they only need two yards for a first down," B.G. warned, becoming worried. "They could get into kicking range for a field goal on this next play."

"We'd better think of something real fast," Sharpy anxiously blurted out.

"How would a little grease on the ball would work?" B.G. asked, thinking out loud.

"That would make the old pigskin fun to handle," Sharpy said.

"Probably more fun than watching someone catch a greased pig," Birdy added with a laugh.

The team got set and the ball was snapped to Thompson. B.G. stretched out his arms at the ball and wiggled his fingers. The ball squirted out of Thompson's hands and sent players from both teams into a mad scramble to recover it. The ball kept squirting out of one player's hands after another until a Falcon fell on the ball and downed it for the Falcons.

The Falcon team started jumping up and down and slapping each other with high fives. Their enthusiasm started spreading to the fans. They were starting to see the game not as a comedy show, but as a chance for the underdog to win.

An old man stood up in the grandstand, shaking his fist and shouting, "That's it, Falcons! <u>Stick</u> it to "em! <u>Give</u> 'em <u>the green finger</u>!"

The Falcon offensive team ran out onto the field excited at this new turn of events and good luck. Sharpy was standing close to one of the referees when the Falcons downed the ball. The referee started blowing his whistle.

Sharpy muttered to himself, "Damn it! Quit blowing that noisy thing! I hate whistles."

Sharpy wiggled his fingers at the whistle. It let out a blast like a foghorn! The referee jumped as if he had been shocked, surprise registering on his face. He slowly took the whistle from his mouth and examined it. Satisfied it was all right, he put it back in his mouth and blew it again. This time an ear-shattering blast like a diesel horn came out, scaring the referee. He jerked the whistle from his mouth, threw it to the ground, and vigorously stomped on it several times.

"When this damned crazy game is over, I'm going to see my psychiatrist!" the referee angrily growled.

"I think I need to see him too," the assistant referee stated.

"Then we'll both go!"

The ball was set on the Mustang's forty-six-yard line. On the first down, Elrod threw an incomplete pass. On the second down, Elrod tried to run around the end but was stopped at the line of scrimmage. With a long pass into the end zone on the third down, the Falcons scored another touchdown. The kicking team came out, and the kick for the extra point was good. The Scoreboard showed the Falcons twenty-one and the Mustangs twenty-seven.

The Falcon fans were going wild with excitement at the prospect of their team winning. An excited Falcon fan leaned over to his friend and happily exclaimed, "If we could just get another touchdown, we could win!"

"Fat chance of that, seeing as how the Mustangs will receive the ball on the kickoff," grumbled his friend. "They'll stall the ball so the time runs out."

The first TV announcer said, "This game is all but over, fans. It's a cinch the Mustangs will keep the ball in bounds so they don't kill the clock."

"The Falcons had better pray for a miracle if they want to win this game," the second announcer added.

"The Falcons may not have much of a chance to win, with so little time left on the clock, but they sure have fired up the fans. Just listen to that roar," the third announcer commented. The announcers did not say any more but simply let the TV listeners at home hear the roar and see the fans standing and shouting for the Falcons.

On the kickoff, the Falcon kicker sent the ball high and a long way down the field. This gave the Falcon team time to run down the field and keep the Mustangs from making any yardage. Two Falcon tacklers pounced on the receiver, and the ball was downed on the Mustang's twenty-one-yard line. The Mustangs did not make any headway on their first two downs. They would have to make ten yards on their third down or they would be forced to kick.

"I always wanted to tackle one of those big guys, just for the fun of it," Birdy said with a devilish smile.

"You'd better get that idea out of your head! You try tackling one of those big bruisers and you'll get yourself hurt real bad," B.G. cautioned.

On the third down, Thompson made a quick, short pass to Naccarato, one of his receivers.

"Naccarato is my man! I'm going to tackle him," Birdy stated with a big smile.

As Naccarato ran down the sideline, Birdy rushed to intercept him. When Birdy got close to him, he shut his eyes and spread his arms out wide to make the tackle.

Birdy missed Naccarato and tackled one of the cheerleaders. Naccarato would have gone all the way for a touchdown if it had not been for Sharpy jerking his pants down, making him fall and lose the ball. The Falcon that was chasing Naccarato downed the ball for the Falcons.

Birdy was lying on the ground smiling, with the stunned cheerleader cradled in his arm when B.G. and Sharpy arrived.

"Just what the hell do you think you're doing, tackling a cheerleader?" B.G. angrily barked.

"I guess I took your advice about getting hurt. This is a lot better," Birdy admitted, stroking the cheerleader.

"Stop horsing around with that gal and get back on the job! We've got a game to salvage!" B.G. ordered angrily.

Birdy gave the girl a big hug and a kiss before getting up. The stunned cheerleader was dizzy and confused by the invisible tackle, hug, and kiss. She wiped her lips and shook her head before slowly getting to her feet.

Recovering the ball was the lucky break the Falcons would desperately need if they were going to have any hope of winning this game. The Falcon's team was delirious with joy, and the fans were standing and shouting, "Falcons! <u>Falcons!</u> Falcons!" as they stomped their feet.

B.G. motioned for his pals to come over to him. They quickly floated over and went into a huddle to figure out their next strategy.

"We've got to figure out something real fast to stop the Mustangs before they win this turkey," B.G. warned.

"If we don't stop them, they're going to cook our goose," Sharpy added.

"I'm out of ideas," Birdy said, shrugging his shoulders.

"I just got an idea! What do you guys think about a swarm of bees?" B.G. asked with a mischievous smile.

"Good idea. We haven't tried that yet," Sharpy agreed.

"Yeah!" Birdy said, waving his pitchfork around. "You keep those little hummers flying while Sharpy and I do a little tickling with these oversized salad forks."

With a fiendish smile on his face, B.G. extended his arms and wiggled his fingers. From out of nowhere a swarm of bees descended on the Mustangs. They started dancing up and down as they swatted at the bees. Some of the players rolled on the ground while they furiously swung their helmets and slapped themselves. Birdy and Sharpy ran around, jabbing the players, making them yell, jump, and swing their arms and stomp their feet. The announcers in the broadcast booth were completely confused about what was going on.

"The Mustangs must have gone around the bend," the first announcer said, jamming his binoculars in his eyes.

"Maybe they're trying some new type of psychology on the Falcons, trying to psyche them out," the second announcer suggested.

"Looks to me like they've got a weedeater loose in their Fruit of the Looms," the third announcer said with a chuckle.

"Whatever is going on sure has the Falcons confused. They're just standing there gawking at the Mustangs and their antics," the first announcer added.

An illusion can last only a short time, so the bees disappeared as quickly as they came. The Mustang players soon discovered that the bees were gone and they had not actually been stung. The referee spotted the ball on the Falcon forty-seven-yard line.

After a quick huddle, The Falcons hurried back to the scrimmage line. In a last desperate attempt to score, Elrod threw a long pass to Morris, who ran it into the end zone for a touchdown. The fans went wild, stomping their feet and yelling for the Falcons. The Scoreboard showed the score tied at twenty-seven.

"It looks like the underdog has come up to tie the game. Now they have a chance to win, if they can make the extra point," the first announcer said.

"The Falcons were expected to lose without Leonard, their star quarterback, "the second announcer added.

"Everyone loves to see the underdog come out on top," the first announcer agreed. "The fans' enthusiasm sure has been building throughout this second half, and now in the last few seconds of the game they are rooting for the Falcons. Just listen to that crowd."

All the fans were standing, stomping their feet, shaking their fists, and shouting "Go, <u>Falcons,</u> go! Go, <u>Falcons,</u> go! Go, <u>Falcons,</u> go!

"The Falcons coming from so far behind sure has everyone fired up," the third announcer said.

"This game is sure to be long remembered," the first announcer said, putting his binoculars up to his eyes again. "It looks like they're sending in Harvey again to kick for the extra point. So far he has kicked three for three, but there is a lot of pressure on him at this crucial moment. This kick will make or lose them a chance for the play-offs."

"Just hope the pressure doesn't get to Harvey. I sure wouldn't want to be under that kind of pressure," the third announcer commented.

"The teams are on the line and it looks like Gilmore is going to hold the ball," the first announcer stated. "There's the snap...Gilmore dropped it!...he sets it... it's a rushed kick...Oh no! The ball is going wide."

When Sharpy saw that the ball was going to miss the goal posts, he waved his hand. The ball made an abrupt hook in the air and sailed through the uprights. The fans were overjoyed and out of control with excitement. Across the field, the Scoreboard showed Falcons twenty-eight and Mustangs twenty-seven.

The Falcon team was jumping up an down and giving each other slaps and hugs. They hoisted

Harvey up on their shoulders and started off the field with him. Mitch was so overjoyed he ran out on the field and pulled Harvey off the shoulders of the players. He gave Harvey a big bear hug.

"You <u>son of</u> a gun!" Mitch shouted. "How in heaven's name did you ever kick a hooked ball?"

"It was that good spring water," Harvey replied, winking at Elrod. "I hid my water bottle when you had the water dumped and I took a big drink before going out to kick."

"Hot damn!" Mitch exclaimed. "I knew that good spring water would clear heads and sharpen wits, and that proves it. From now on we're taking barrels of that spring water with us wherever we go."

Gradually the stadium began to clear, and it was not long before it was quiet and empty—except for the three lone figures standing in the middle of the field. The three had silly grins on their faces and obviously quite pleased with their mischievous accomplishments. It wasn't long before Satan appeared before them.

"W-e-l-l, judging by the looks on those smug faces, I'd say you're very pleased with yourselves," Satan said.

"We sure are. You owe each of us a hundred point for this game," B.G. stated proudly.

"We should get the maximum for all the hard work waving our hands and wiggling our fingers," Birdy added.

"We sure caused a lot of swearing and explosive tempers, and we even got old Valletta for you," B.G. said.

"Hold it! Just hold it right there. I don't have Vallette yet, and as for the other things, I'll have to consult the computer," Satan informed.

Satan waved his hand and the computer materialized before him. He started flipping switches and pressing buttons while the three advocates watched.

"Ah, here we are," Satan said, pausing to study the screen. "B.G. for starting the fight between the two fans and for causing O'Malley to lose his temper…you get five credits."

"Credits, hell! I should get a lot of points. Credits don't count up fast enough. How about some heavy points for Valletta?"

"I said I don't have Valletta yet. He'll be coming along soon, and when he does, Sharpy will get twenty points."

"Bull crap! That was a joint effort, and each of us should get a hundred points."

"Now ain't that hell," Satan mocked. "Sharpy was the one that found out about Valletta, so he gets the points."

"That stinks," B.G. grumbled to Birdy. "I think the two of us just got diddled again by the green finger."

"How about me?" Birdy asked.

Satan pressed more buttons on the computer and then studied the screen, "Oh, yes…the boy eating popcorn and dumping his drink in his father's lap. For that you get four credits."

"Four lousy credits? I should get a lot more than that," Birdy protested.

Ignoring Birdy's protest, Satan continued, "As for the two drunks during the half-time intermission, you lose your credits, and the computer is wiped clean."

Lose my four lousy credits! Why?" Birdy blurted in anger.

"You were having more fun than you were causing trouble!" Satan replied.

"But all those pink elephants, floating beer, and a green snake slithering out of the bottle, "Birdy added, continuing to protest.

"The way I see it," Satan said, cocking his head and thinking, "All you did was interrupt a damned good drinking party. Besides, I like drunks. They do such wonderfully mean things when they're under the influence."

"But—but—I," Birdy stammered.

"No buts about it! I make the rules and call the shots. No credit. Now, for the football game," Satan said, pausing to light a cigar and study the computer screen, "You three caused a little confusion, no fights, and very little swearing. Therefore, I'll be generous and give each of you three points.

"That sucks!" B.G. said angrily. "We're never going to get out of this damned mess at this rate."

"I said it wouldn't be easy getting a hundred points. Would you rather go back?" Satan asked.

"Hell no!" B.G. replied. "We'll try again someplace else."

"Let's get our asses out of here before that lying weasel takes away any more points," Sharpy suggested, his anger rising.

"Yeah! It sounds like we just got the <u>green finger</u> again," B.G. growled.

Birdy and Sharpy turned and walked away toward the exit. B.G. ran and caught up with them.

"Hold it, you guys." B.G. said.

"If Satan is so damned smart and it's his game, why don't we let him tell us where to go to get the most points?"

"Do you think we can trust the bastard?" Birdy asked.

"Yes, that old chiseling son of a bitch should help us," Sharpy growled.

"I heard that," Satan shouted. "Calling me names is not going to help your cause. You don't go around biting the hand that feeds you."

"Feed us!" Birdy repeated. "It's more like the hand that keeps giving us the green finger."

"It's just a matter of interpretation," Satan replied smugly.

"Yeah, just look who's doing the interpreting," Birdy commented glumly.

It's my game, and I call it the way I see it," Satan replied, puffing on his cigar. "So you want to know where to go next to get the most points? I would go to one of the large cities if it were me."

"We don't want to go to any big city. They're bad enough without our help," B.G. replied.

"Just how are we going to get points for things they already do?" Sharpy asked.

"That's easy. Just help them do more of whatever they're doing, and you'll get your points," Satan coolly replied.

"That sounds easy enough. Okay, big cities, here we come. Let's take a look at them, and then pick one," B.G. suggested.

The three devil's advocates started across the playing field toward the exit, talking. Gradually they started to fade and finally disappeared.

"I still don't trust him. It all sounds too easy. There has to be a catch someplace," Sharpy grumbled.

"I think that's how he gets his jollies, by giving us the green finger and sticking it to us," Birdy stated.

THE END

ABOUT THE AUTHOR

The author grew up in Indiana and graduated from Ball State University, served in the military and taught school for thirty-five years. Since retiring he spends most of his time writing novels, screenplays and teleplays. Any free time is spent golfing and fishing.